PROTECTING LOVE

SAINTS PROTECTION & INVESTIGATIONS

MARYANN JORDAN

Cover design: Cosmic Letterz

ISBN ebook: 978-1-947214-19-4

ISBN print: 978-1-947214-18-7

❀ Created with Vellum

The loud banging coming from the garage had Mrs. Cartwright heading out to see what was causing the commotion. *Who am I kidding?* She grinned. *I know exactly what I'll find.* Sure enough, as she rounded the corner and peeked into the garage, she saw her son, Patrick, and her father. Her tow-headed son's head was bent forward, almost touching the gray of his grandfather's. The two sat on low, wooden stools on the concrete floor, pieces of what used to be a lawnmower strewn all about. It appeared the machine was in the process of being taken apart or being put back together —she could not tell. The metal parts were lined meticulously in what appeared to be a pattern. Leaning against the doorframe, the evening sun warmed her back as it cast a glow on the garage's inhabitants, and she listened as her father patiently explained the process of putting the lawnmower back together.

Twelve-year-old Patrick loved the idea of taking things apart and seeing how they worked. How the intricate pieces fit together perfectly to make something amazing. And then the process of building something from scratch, with his grandfather's guidance, was a dream come true.

"You've got to understand each part and how it works in the whole," Gramps said, picking up part of the small engine. "You can't rush...these things take time to make sure they fit together just right." The two bent their heads down toward the blueprint lying on the floor next to their legs.

Patrick wiped his face with the back of his hand, still managing to leave a smudge of oil across his cheek. His blue eyes focused on Gramps, memorizing every move he made as he recreated the machine. Breaker points. Condenser. Crankcase. Carburetor.

"Reminds me of your grandma and me," Gramps said, chuckling. "Weren't no love at first sight, I'll tell you."

Turning his eyes up to his grandfather, Patrick's mouth hung open. His grandfather often talked about life when they were working, but he had never heard him speak about grandma in any other terms than lovingly.

"Saw her at a church picnic in the park one afternoon. Me and my buddies came roaring into town in our farm trucks, saw a bunch of purdy girls and headed straight over to them. A few of them girls started giving my friends the eye, but the one that caught mine was a tall blonde. She wouldn't give rough ol' me the time of day, sticking her snooty nose in the air. So I figured I didn't need her and made the moves on another one.

Found out later, the purdy blonde was the preacher's daughter."

"Grandma was mean to you just because of the way you looked?" Patrick asked, his young mind working to grapple the intricacies of the story.

"Naw, your grandma was good as gold. But I found out later, she knew her daddy woulda had a fit if his girl was flirtin' at the church picnic with little kids running around. And with a bunch of guys that rolled up into town, loud and rowdy, barging into the park."

"So what happened?" Patrick asked, picking up the air filter cover and fitting the lid carefully back on after inserting the air filter inside.

His grandfather cleaned the spark plugs and lifted his eyes to his grandson, a smile dancing on his lips. "Well, just like this lawnmower, your grandmother and I had to work to make sure the parts went together. I learned that she was really shy and was overwhelmed when me and my buddies rolled up. She was afraid that her daddy wouldn't like me and assumed we wouldn't be a good fit. We had just come in from the farm...hot, sweaty, and dirty. I wasn't doin' myself any favors by not gettin' cleaned up. So the next weekend, I got all spruced up, drove right up to your grandma's house and knocked on the front door."

Eyes wide, Patrick stopped what he was doing, eager to hear the rest of the story.

Inserting the clean spark plugs, his grandfather was quiet for several minutes as they finished putting the motor back together. "Well, just like working on this piece of equipment, I learned that I needed patience and

MARYANN JORDAN

care to build somethin' with your grandmother. It wasn't gonna happen overnight. And she learned that underneath the rough exterior, was the heart of a man who'd love her for the rest of her life."

Grinning, Patrick interrupted, "And then you got married?"

Chuckling, Gramps shook his head. "Nah. It took about six months of courtin' her, getting to know her, and us makin' sure we were a good fit. Not fast...not instant. But slow and sure. Then we got married and I knew we were building something strong."

Looking down at the lawnmower, now complete with all of its parts put back together, they stood. "You think we can see if it's time to check 'er out?"

Nodding enthusiastically, Patrick grinned, eager to see the end results of their afternoon project.

Bending over, Gramps primed the engine a few times before grabbing the starter handle and giving it a strong pull. The motor sputtered a time or two before firing up with a roar. Patrick clapped his hands in glee, pride settling through his young frame. Letting it run a moment, Gramps then turned off the motor and grinned down at his grandson.

"Gotta build it, make sure the parts fit together just right...then it's a thing of beauty."

"Then we're all done?" Patrick asked, accomplishment showing in his face.

"Naw, naw," Gramps answered, chuckling as his grandson's face fell. "You gotta treat it right. Protect it. Cherish it. Take real good care of it, or it can fall apart on you. And then it takes even longer to put back together again."

Patrick had no idea if his grandfather was talking about the motor...or something more personal...but it did not matter. He had helped build something and it worked. And the feeling was incredible.

"All right, you two," his mother called from the doorway. "Time for supper. Go get washed up."

Patrick ran ahead and scrubbed the grease from his hands and face before moving back into the kitchen. He watched as his grandfather came in, stopping at the wheelchair where his grandmother sat. The stroke made movement difficult, but her blue eyes sparkled as much as ever. His grandfather bent over, touching his wife's cheek before planting a soft kiss on her smooth skin. "Love you, darlin' girl," he whispered, gaining a lopsided smile in return as she patted his hand.

Patrick had seen these endearments many times before, but after hearing his grandfather's story, he halted in his rush to go to the table. *It takes time to make sure these things fit. Patience and care to build something. Slow and sure. And protect it to keep it strong.*

In a moment of clarity, twelve-year-old Patrick knew he had been taught a powerful lesson—one that would stay with him forever. Taking a deep breath, he pushed himself off the wall and moved into the room, kissing his grandmother also.

His mother watched from the other side of the room...a smile on her face.

Ten Years Later

Graduating with an Engineering degree, Patrick walked through the crowd looking for his family. The cute, tow-headed boy had grown into a handsome man, turning heads as he walked by. Taller than most, his blue eyes searched easily over the sea of mortarboards, finally spotting the familiar blonde hair of his sister, Angel. Making his way to them, he scooped her up into a hug as she gleefully congratulated him. Next, his mother and father offered their heartfelt congratulations as well. Turning, he clasped the arthritic hand of his grandfather who pulled him into a hug, clapping him on the back. His grandmother had passed, but Patrick knew she was here in spirit.

Later, at the restaurant where the family celebrated, his grandfather quieted the exuberant group. The lines in his face deepened as he smiled over the gathering. Holding up his glass of beer, he cleared his throat.

"It'll be a while before we're all together again, so I figure I might as well say a few words. Son," he said, facing Patrick, "you're leaving in a couple of days for boot camp and then OCS. You'll make a fine Army officer with the Corps of Engineers. I'd like to think that them days of us putterin' around in the workshop helped get you where you are today."

The others at the table chuckled, remembering many take-it-apart-only-to-put-it-back-together projects.

Gramps continued, "But I know your love of building didn't just come from me. I know you can't wear it in the military, but I'd like to give you a little something to remember me by." He reached into his pocket and pulled out a St. Patrick medallion on a silver chain. "This here saint is the patron saint of Engineers. Want you to have it and to remember that it takes time, patience, and care to build something. And I'm not only talkin' about machines. But relationships as well."

Patrick blinked several times battling the tears he felt stinging the back of his eyes. His grandfather had never regained the bright twinkle in his eyes after his wife passed away and Patrick knew that the many years of them together, building a marriage and family, had taken the time and patience his grandfather spoke of.

"So go with God and your family's blessing. And when you find the right one, work to build it right and protect it to keep it strong."

2

SIX YEARS LATER

Patrick left the Corps of Engineers base near Sacramento, California, and headed to his jeep. *Thank God, it's Friday.* Climbing into his vehicle, he sat for a moment in indecision before heading to the bar. Needing to unwind, he hoped he would run into some friends to share a beer and pass some time with.

Walking into the old establishment, he headed to the bar. The Army had honed his body, now taller and more muscular than ever. Ordering dinner, he settled in at a tall table with his beer until his food came out. Slowly, the stress of the day slipped away and he began to relax. Hearing his name called out from behind him, he swiveled around on his bar stool. Seeing the large man walking in, he grinned, lifting his hand in greeting.

Clasping hands, Patrick pulled Chris Todd in for a man hug. "Hoped I'd find you here on a Friday afternoon," he admitted.

"Hell, you shoulda just called me," Chris replied. "I was excited to hear that you were going to be stationed here for a while." He settled onto the bar stool next to Patrick's and nodded toward the bartender.

"Well, I've only got four more months in and then... aw, hell, who knows what'll I do at that time."

Chris took a long pull on his beer before setting the bottle down, the water droplets sliding off the glass and onto the surface of the bar. "Yeah, it sucks trying to figure out what the fuck to do when you get out."

The two men met under unlikely circumstances when on tour in Afghanistan. Patrick, a member of the Corps of Engineers, had been working on building bridges that would withstand some of the crude explosives that a few villages were using. He worked with several Special Forces squads, continuing to train the Engineer Sergeants. The Army contracted with the SEALS and used some of their Explosive Ordnance Disposal teams to assist in testing. Patrick and Chris hit it off, both respecting each other's work. Finding the time to share beers, poker games, and whenever possible pick-up basketball games, their acquaintance grew into a friendship.

Chris, injured on a mission, now resided in California after obtaining a medical discharge. The big man smiled at Patrick and said, "Don't reckon you've heard... but I'm married now."

Patrick, in the middle of a bite of his hamburger, stopped suddenly, turning to face his friend. "No kiddin'?" Tossing down his food, he wiped his hands before slapping Chris on the back. "Congratulations, man. That's great news!"

Chris's food delivered, the two men settled in to eat,

talk, and reminisce. After finishing and pushing his plate back, Chris asked, "So what are you thinking about doing?"

Patrick leaned his tall body back on the stool, hearing the wooden legs creak. "Don't know. Love building things...the Army gave me the chance to not only design what was needed but to go out in the field and actually get my hands on it as well. Most civil engineering jobs I've looked at would have me sitting at a desk all day. I mean, I'd be able to go out to the sites, but I'd be observing."

"I hear you," Chris replied. "When I was first injured, I thought it might be the end of my career as a SEAL." He held up his hand, complete with missing fingers and mangled scars. "Thank God it didn't."

"I heard about that, and am really sorry that happened to you," Patrick said, shaking his head. He had known many servicemen injured in the war, and the loss was almost always life changing.

"I woulda hated sitting behind a desk also."

"I don't have time to do another tour so I got sent here to do a desk job procuring materials." He caught Chris's dubious expression and chuckled. "Yeah, it's about as exciting as it sounds. I sit behind a desk, ordering shit then checking it when it comes in."

"You have to keep track of where the shipments go? I know there's always thefts of military equipment," Chris commented. "You have any of that with what you're working on?"

"Not that I've seen, but then I'm just dealing with building materials. Concrete, steel, mostly geotechnical.

Honestly, boring as shit, but I'll be out in four months and then I'll figure out what I'm going to do."

"Thinking of staying in California?"

"Got family in Virginia so I'll probably head east to visit with them when I get out. Whether or not I stay, well…I'll decide then."

"If I recall, you've got a hot-as-fuck sister there, don't you?"

Laughing, Patrick nodded. "Little sis grew up. She got her business degree and is a baker. Owns her own business and bakes cupcakes for a living, if you can believe that!" Almost as an afterthought, he added, "She's engaged now to a former FBI agent. He works for a private security investigation company now. Met his boss, Jack Bryant, former Special Forces. I was impressed with what he was doing." Chuckling again, he said, "The man all but offered me a job when I met him."

"Think you'd like to do that?" Chris asked. "Got to tell you, my SEAL team and I have had some great missions and the investigating aspect is especially interesting."

"Don't know," Patrick answered honestly. "Guess I'll just have to wait and see."

The silence settled comfortably over the two men, as they finished their beers. The waitress hung around the table for a few minutes after delivering the next round, shooting hopeful smiles his way. He glanced at her appreciatively—long, blonde hair, tits and ass abundantly displayed, an expression of expectation on her face. *Nothing. Don't feel a goddamn thing.* After a minute, she turned on her heels and flounced away, a pout replacing the smile and her stomp indicating her indignation.

Laughing, Chris commented, "Looks like you weren't in the mood tonight."

"Nah," Patrick agreed, running his hand over his short hair. He was thoughtful for a moment before adding, "Remember the feeling you got when you first became a SEAL and felt like you had just been given a pussy-magnet badge?" Hearing Chris's chuckle and seeing his nod, he grinned back. "But I swear, for a while now, I'm just not interested in tapping that anymore."

"Yeah, well, when you find the right one, you'll know it and then you'll definitely never wonder about anyone else again."

Smiling appreciatively at his friend, Patrick noticed the genuinely relaxed expression on Chris's face. "Glad you got that, man. Hope to meet her sometime."

"Absolutely," Chris nodded enthusiastically, standing to leave. The two men said goodbye with promises to get together soon and then Chris left. Patrick finished his beer, left a good tip and nodded to the bartender as he walked out. The waitress had given him one last pouty invitation that he ignored. The sense of longing deep inside his chest simply intensified, but he knew she was not the one to take it away.

Evelyn Sinclair's heels tapped out a rhythm on the tile floor of the hall between her office and the conference room. Stopping just outside the door, where a decorative mirror was hanging over a small table, she smoothed her skirt and glanced down to make sure her blouse was perfect. *Good, dropping my sandwich at lunch didn't leave a spot.* Running her hand over her dark brown hair, making sure the stray hairs were in place, she glanced at her subtle makeup. It was hard presenting a polished, professional appearance without drawing attention to her sexuality. *One of the many difficult things about being a woman in a man's field.* She was not surprised—the same thing had happened in college. Even in this day and age of enlightenment, there were few women in the geotechnical degree programs. Standing up straight, she walked into the meeting.

Sliding into a seat after pouring herself a cup of coffee, she smiled at the others coming in. While it may be a man's world, she had to admit that she enjoyed the other employees...for the most part. Norman Oysten, the owner and president of Geotechnical Manufacturing Systems, along with his oldest son, Gary, as vice president, ran a top-notch company that managed to be employee friendly. The younger son, Saul, was head of the Financial and Accounting Department.

Sipping her coffee, her eyes landed on the last person to enter the room, his ever-present glower firmly in place. Ed Snyder plopped in the seat next to her, then glanced at the coffee in her hand.

"Any more of that?" he asked, his voice sounding like an order instead of a question.

"Yes, over on the credenza where it always is," Evelyn replied evenly. Forcing the grimace from her face, she caught the grin from Saul across the table. Ed grunted as he hefted himself up and over to the coffee, and she returned Saul's grin. Ed had been slow to accept Evelyn and she knew that he would continue to treat her as an assistant if she allowed him to.

The meeting soon came to order and she concentrated on taking specific notes.Having only been working at GMS for a few months, she still felt as though she needed to prove herself. But, as usual, she was well prepared and when called upon to answer questions, she was professional and succinct.

Evelyn applied at GMS, a national leader in geotechnical materials, for an engineering job, but a position would not be available until one of their current engineers retired. She had been promised that would be within six months and she decided to take them up on their offer of working in the military sales department until then. *If it had been any other company but GMS, I'd never be doing this,* she thought as the meeting droned on. But Norman and Gary wanted her—a woman geotechnical engineer was not easy to find and the need for diversity was a point in her favor. Plus her credentials were perfect. Gary convinced her that starting for a few months in sales would allow her to see exactly where her designs would be used in the real world, something many Engineers did not get to observe.

"That'll do for today," Norman finally announced, adding, "I hope everyone has a good weekend."

Weekend...yes! A chance to relax! Not that she had any plans, but Evelyn used her weekends as a chance to recharge her batteries before hitting the work-week once more. She watched as Ed stomped out of the meeting, his usual demeanor still intact.

"Hey, girlie, why don't you get me some coffee?" Saul asked, his voice barely containing his mirth.

Pretending to spear him with a glower, her laughter forced its way out. "You know, it's not that I'd mind getting someone coffee if I was standing next to it getting my own, but I swear that man lives in the dark ages!"

"I know," Saul agreed. "I just had to tease you, though."

Walking over, Gary grinned. "I wish you could have seen your face, Evelyn. It was priceless."

The three started to walk out when Norman stopped them. He stepped up to her and laid his hand on her arm. "You mustn't mind Ed too much. He's a good plant manager...if a little rough around the edges. But never doubt, Ms. Sinclair, you are a valued team member here at GMS. We were thrilled to get you."

Warming at his praise, she thanked him. "I love working here," she admitted. *But I really hate sales and can't wait until I get the engineering position!*

The group walked out of the conference room, each heading to their offices to pack up for the weekend. As she made her way to her car, she lifted her face to the spring sun, feeling the freedom that only comes with a Friday afternoon.

Evelyn stretched out on the lawn chair next to the pool at her condo complex, thrilled to have nabbed one of the nice, spacious condos to rent from owners who had to go out of the country for two years. It came furnished and, while not cheap, she found that her salary from GMS offered her the luxury of being able to afford it. The gym and pool were bonuses...*okay, so I never go to the gym*, she thought ruefully, looking down at her curves. Glancing at several of the other young women with their trim, athletic bodies, she thought, *perhaps I should make an effort to make it to the gym.*

Having spent Saturday morning cleaning and then grocery shopping, she closed her eyes, allowing the warmth of the sun to seep into her body as she drifted off to sleep. Several minutes later, the tittering of the girls sitting close to her woke her up. Looking over, she saw what was causing the commotion. Several men, each chiseled and tan, walked by, heading to the condo's volleyball sandpit.

One of the men turned his face toward them, his gaze, hidden behind reflector sunglasses, appeared to roam over the women in a cursory manner until landing—and holding—on her. *Damn*, she thought as she met his perusal. Tall, muscular arms and legs, sandy-blond hair, square jaw. Unable to discern his eye color, she found herself staring at his reflective glasses. *I guess trim isn't his cup of tea.* A smile played on the corners of her lips before he reached up and jerked his t-shirt over his head. *Double damn.* His chest and ripped stomach muscles were just as defined as his arms and thighs. Around his neck hung two chains. One with some kind of medallion and the other...dog tags. *Military. Just my luck...I see someone interesting and they're a soldier.*

Evelyn had nothing against the military—she had been an Army brat herself. But years of having to start over in school every two to three years and she swore she would never put her children through that. For some, it was great. Her outgoing older sister loved it, but for her? The shy, smart girl never felt like she had time to fit in or make friends.

Sliding her sunglasses back down on her face, she leaned her head back, dismissing any thoughts of the handsome soldier still staring at her.

———

Patrick, glad to get the call on Saturday to join some friends for a few games at their condo, had noticed the women lying in the sun. A group of athletic women caught his eyes first as he walked by, but it was the stunning woman sitting by herself that had him looking twice.

A curvy figure showcased in a black one-piece swimsuit, her long brown hair cascading down her back, red highlights glinting in the sunshine. And she was staring back at him appreciatively. Her sunglasses were pushed up on her head and he considered walking straight over to her to introduce himself as he jerked his t-shirt off.

Her gaze moved up and down him, seemingly interested until landing on his chest. Then she slid her glasses down and leaned her head back, no longer gazing at him. *Wow, that's a brushoff,* he thought ruefully. His hand moved up, fingering the St. Patrick medallion. *It's just as well, Gramps. I don't have enough time to build something carefully now anyway.*

With that, he jogged over to his friends and began the game. Looking over several minutes later, he noticed the chair was empty and the beauty nowhere in sight.

3

Patrick walked his report down the hall to his supervisor's office. "Major Trumble? I need you to take a look at this and let me know what you want me to do, Sir."

The Major looked up, immediately taking the report from the young Captain's hand. "Is there a problem?"

"Yes, Sir. The latest shipment from GMS appears to be missing some of the order. I filed the requisite claim with them, but they're disputing the discrepancy. They have the shipping order from their end that was signed off by their sales division and their plant manager. On our end, we're missing half a truckload of the transoms and side panels for the latest Bailey bridge order."

The Major took several minutes to read over Patrick's report and then looked up, nodding. "All right, I'll suggest you take a trip to GMS and see if you can handle the discrepancy issue in person. It would normally be difficult, but with them in the Sacramento area, you can easily handle that. We will brief tomorrow before you meet with them."

Accepting the assignment, he walked back to his office. Sitting at his desk, he leaned back in his chair, closing his eyes for a moment allowing the sun streaming through the window to warm his face. Sucking in a deep breath, he turned his attention back to his computer. Geotechnical Manufacturing Systems. He moved through their website, finding the email of his contact. *Evelyn Sinclair. Geotechnical Engineer. Military Sales.*

He imagined the woman he would be meeting with. Dark hair...probably grey. Perhaps fuzzy. Thick Glasses. Sensible dark slacks and white blouse. And loafers...or pumps.

Giving himself a mental shake, he rubbed his hand over his face. *What a prick thought,* he chastised himself, sitting up in his chair and composing the professional email requesting the meeting. When in college, the Engineering School was certainly not a place to meet women when only about fifteen percent of the class was made up of females. *Well, hopefully, we can call a quick meeting and they will acquiesce to our demands for the lost items to be replaced.*

He received a response from her quickly and the meeting was scheduled for the day after tomorrow. Nodding, he felt more at ease. *Good, the last thing I want is to end my Army career with a problem...or a complication.*

Evelyn closed her computer for the day but left her office a little early planning to stop by Saul's office on her way out. They had created an easy friendship, including a little innocent flirting on his side and she had carefully let him know she did not date co-workers. Sticking her head in, she nodded as he held up a finger indicating he was almost finished with his conference call.

"Hey," he called out, grinning as she entered. "What's up?"

"I forwarded a claim to you and wanted you to know that I've accepted a meeting with the Army's representative on Wednesday."

"I saw that," he said, concern crossing his expression. "What do you think's going on?"

"I've got no idea. I'll talk to Ed tomorrow to find out who signed off on the shipment when it left and make sure we have our ducks in a row before the meeting."

Saul nodded, then checked his calendar. "I've got a meeting myself on Wednesday, but I can move it if you want me there."

She cocked her head to the side in question.

He looked up, saw the look on her face and immediately said, "No, no, I don't mean to imply you can't handle it. I just thought if you'd like my presence, I'd be glad to—"

"Glad to what?" Gary asked, moving past Evelyn into his brother's office.

She opened her mouth to explain, but Saul spoke first. "There's been a claim sent in from the Army Corps of Engineers. They claim part of the shipment was missing. They have requested a meeting this Wednesday with Evelyn."

Gary turned around, saying, "You want me to be there too?"

Throwing her hands up in the air, she chastised her bosses. "Thanks for the vote of confidence, guys. I think little ol' me can handle the big, bad, Army Captain."

The two brothers grinned, both having the sense to blush as she put them in their place. "Sorry," Gary and Saul said in unison, then looked at each other and laughed.

Grinning as well, she stepped the rest of the way into Saul's office and sat down with them. The two looked like brothers and both younger versions of their father. Almost black hair, cut fairly short and swept to the side. Gary was a bit bulkier while Saul was a couple inches taller. The three sat and chatted amicably for a few minutes before Gary stood to leave.

"How's Sandra?" Evelyn asked.

"She's great," Gary answered. "Only a month to go and I'll hold my son."

Smiling, she replied, "Well, tell her I said hello. I've got a baby gift for you…I'll bring it to you next week."

Nodding, he started to walk away then stopped and turned at the door. "Evelyn, what do you think about the Army's claim?"

"I've emailed Ed…" she began, hating the feeling she always got when having to deal with the surly plant manager. "He says the shipment was personally overseen by him and it was fine when it left our plant. I'm going over to talk to him tomorrow."

She held Gary's gaze, steeling herself. *I won't let them*

see that I'm intimidated by the man. Gary then gave her a satisfied nod and walked out of the office.

Turning back to Saul, she said, "What do you think?"

"I don't know, Evelyn. My office handles the finances and billing…not the shipments themselves."

"Oh, I know," she rushed to say. "I just mean about everything."

"Well, Ed's worked here for a long time and I can't imagine him suddenly not doing his job correctly. But… on the other hand, I hardly think the Army is trying to scam us." He leaned back in his seat before adding, "At least I hope they aren't. You'll have to let me know what you think about the Army representative they send."

As she walked out of his office, he called out, "And you'll have to let me know if I need to be jealous!" leaving her to wonder if he were teasing or serious.

Wednesday morning came and Evelyn found herself unusually nervous. *This is ridiculous,* she chastised herself. *He's not the first client I've met with or had to deal with.* But she admitted to herself that she hated this part of the job. Hopefully, only a few more months of this and she would finally be in an engineering position and not in sales.

She tried to envision what the Army Captain would look like and hoped she was not dealing with a grumpy old man. After having talked to Ed again, she really wanted to avoid that.

Replaying in her mind the latest conversation she had with the plant manager, she shivered.

Driving to the main manufacturing area, I had parked then walked into the manufacturing building. Moving through the production area, I came to the bottom of the stairs leading to the offices. Having emailed to let him know I was coming, I ignored his response about being too busy to go back over something they had already discussed. Now, I was determined to corner him, just catching him coming out of his office.

He took one look at me, scowled and said, "Don't got time now, Ms. Sinclair."

"Well, make time, Mr. Snyder," I quipped, noting his eyes grew wide at my order and determined he was a little in awe that I had a backbone. Holding his gaze, I quelled the nervousness in my stomach. Disliking confrontation, I hated having to fight for respect even more.

After a tense moment, he jerked his head up in silent response and turned to go back into his office, plopping down heavily in his chair. Following, I sat in the seat opposite, resting my hands in my lap on the folder I had brought with me.

"You seem to think that I'm accusing you of wrongdoing," I began, "but I'm not. I'm just trying to find where the discrepancy came from. Either we did not ship the requisite number of transoms and side panels, or they did not inventory them correctly on their end. Before I meet with the Army representative, I want to make sure I have my facts straight."

"I told you before and I'll tell you again for the last time. Either I, or my second in command, Roger, checks each ship-

ment before it goes out. We sign off, and then the truck driver signs."

"I understand the procedure, Mr. Snyder. What concerns me is that we're missing the signature of one of the drivers and the shipment was missing one fourth of its contents."

"Says the Army guy," Ed bit out.

"I've got the papers right here," I argued back, my voice rising in frustration.

"And I'm tellin' you, my end is straight. I don't hire the fuckin' drivers and if they can't do their fuckin' jobs then that's not on me," he growled, standing with his fists firmly planted on the desk as his large body leaned toward her.

Fighting anger and intimidation, I stood on shaky legs and returned his glare. "Fine, I'll have my meeting today, but without that driver's signature, if the client requests, we'll be sending another shipment and eating the costs." With that, I turned and stalked out of his office, my insides quaking as I made my way back to the staircase.

Now, Evelyn waited anxiously for the Army's representative, Captain Cartwright to appear. She did not have to wait long, as he was on time. The secretary knocked on the conference room door and announced him before stepping back and allowing him entrance.

"Captain Cartwright, what a pleasure to meet—"

The words halted in her mouth as she took in the handsome man, dressed in his military uniform. *The man from the condo pool!* She narrowed her eyes as she took him in. Tall—way over six feet. Trimmed hair, a mixture of brown and sandy blond. Broad shoulders tapering to a slimmer waist. Neat. Proper. Wearing a blue uniform. *Blue?*

Patrick startled as his eyes moved over Evelyn, cocking his head to the side. When he entered the room, he immediately recognized her as the beauty from the pool last weekend. Her rich, brunette hair pulled back into a low ponytail. Her subtle makeup was expertly applied...perfect for the workplace without being too overblown. Her luscious body covered in a fitted, gray, pencil skirt with a slight ruffle at the bottom, paired with a soft pink blouse, pink pearl buttons the only adornment. As his eyes trailed down, he noticed her heels...not sensible pumps, but not the fuck-me variety either. *Perfect. Professional. And utterly—*

"I thought you were from the Army?" she blurted.

Jerking his startled gaze back to hers, he responded, "What? I am. Army Captain Cartwright."

"But you're wearing blue," she stated the obvious.

Smiling, he nodded. "Yes, Ma'am. The U.S. Army has changed the uniform back to blue."

"It used to be blue?" she continued, her questioning gaze holding his own.

"Yes, Ma'am."

No words were spoken for a moment until Evelyn shook herself out of her stupor and thrust her hand forward. *God, I just looked like an idiot!* "I'm very sorry," she apologized. "That was not very professional of me... I...uh...well, I was just startled."

He took her hand, giving it a firm shake, holding her fingers for a few seconds longer than needed. "Startled?"

"Um...yes. At the uniform," she explained, not wanting to admit she remembered seeing him before.

"Ah, the uniform. And here I thought perhaps we had met before," he added smoothly.

"No, no. I don't think so."

"Well, I assure you that if I had met you, I would not forget," he said with a grin, noticing her discomfort. "But I don't believe we finished the introductions."

"Of course," she said, a blush rushing to her cheeks. "I'm very glad to meet you, Captain Cartwright. I'm Evelyn Sinclair."

"Please call me Patrick," he requested.

She heard his request, but it felt more like a gentle order. Cocking her head to the side, she nodded. "All right. And you may call me Evelyn." Determined to take charge of the meeting, she motioned to a chair at the large conference table. "Please have a seat. It will just be the two of us, so I admit the surroundings are a little formal, but we don't have a smaller conference room available at the moment."

They both sat, across from each other, placing their files on the table in front of them. Before she had a chance to speak, Patrick immediately began, opening up the files in front of him.

"As you can see, we inventory the shipments as they come in. From the time stamp, it appears that three of the trucks came in within thirty minutes of each other and the fourth truck did not arrive for another hour and a half."

"Yes, but—"

"As you can also see, the inventory forms were not

initially signed by the last truck driver and the base personnel noted the total when he signed off."

"I underst—"

Tapping his finger down on the papers in front of him, he continued, "We are requesting immediate delivery of the missing shipment as well as a discounted price on the next shipment, due to the overhead of time delay in getting the equipment out to the men in the field."

The silence thundered around the room as the two inhabitants stared at each other...one glaring and one with a steady expression.

"Are you finished?" Evelyn asked, her voice laced with irritation, a slight shaking of her hand the only outward indication of her anger...or nervousness.

"For now," Patrick answered, seemingly surprised at her tone of voice. He realized she had given off a timid vibe when they first met. As beautiful as she was, he also assumed she would be a pushover for his request. Now he gazed across the table and viewed her stiff-back, tight-lipped body language. *Damn, I've pissed her off.*

"We are aware of the facts. I have investigated and found that the truck driver in question was a temporary substitute due to the regular truck driver having called in sick. The signing procedures were overlooked by him. He also became lost in transit. This, of course, is with us and we certainly agree that there is no way to refute the discrepancy—"

"Refute the discrepancy? Why would you need to dispute it? We inventoried and part of the shipment was missing."

"Will you please stop interrupting me!" Evelyn finally managed to bite out, trying to maintain her professionalism in the face of the infuriating man, sitting in front of her, appearing cool and collected.

His eyes held hers as a slow smile curved his lips. Nodding his head to the side, he replied, "I apologize. Of course, proceed."

Looking back down at the papers in front of her, she tried to still her racing pulse. *Damn, why am I so rattled? Jesus, let's just get this meeting over with!* "As I was saying, because proper procedures were not followed on our end, we have no way of validating…or disputing…your information, therefore GMS takes responsibility for the missing items. I have been assured that everything loaded was delivered, but in the interest of good relations, we will have no choice but to take your word."

Leaning back, Patrick studied the flustered woman in front of him. And grinned. *She's even more beautiful up close.*

4

"I guarantee you, my word is sound," Patrick said, holding her gaze, thinking he would love to do nothing more than kiss the irritated expression right off her face. In fact, glancing at the heavy table in front of them, he needed to tamp down the rising hard-on just at the thought of what he would like to do with her on the table.

"Be that as it may, we still need to come to some equitable agreement about how to proceed." Seeing his quirked eyebrow, she plunged on. "GMS is prepared to send out the disputed number of transoms and side panels and that shipment can be guaranteed on this Friday. Our plant manager will be overseeing the shipment and our regular driver will be making the delivery. I have been informed by our Financial Department that we will be able to offer a discount of ten percent to replace the missing items."

Snapping out of his lust-wandering mind, Patrick's eyes jumped back to hers. "Ten percent?"

Refusing to back down, she licked her lips and nodded. "Yes, that is what was given to me."

"To you, it may be a simple oversight, but to us, we had to delay the entire shipment to the field. Delays that cost money, time, and possibly soldiers' lives if we cannot handle the logistics of getting equipment to them. Perhaps that doesn't mean anything to you, but I assure—"

"How dare you assume to know what means something to me," she retorted.

"Well, I can tell you that my superiors will not accept a ten percent discount as a penalty," he argued, leaning forward.

Sitting back, Evelyn wondered how the meeting had become so filled with animosity. *Oh, yeah...he walked in with attitude and has been serving it ever since he sat down! Well, two can play this game.* "Unfortunately, I am unable to offer more at this time without checking with my Finance Department."

"Then I suggest you call them now because we need that shipment."

Pushing her seat backward with force, she stood, slamming her files closed. "If you will wait, I'll see what I can do." Without bothering to look at him, she strode out of the room. Once the door closed behind her, she went to her secretary. "Molly, can you go see if Commander Macho in there needs anything? I've got to get hold of Saul."

Grinning, Molly patted her red curls and jumped up. "Oooh, best assignment you've given me all day!"

Rolling her eyes, Evelyn called Saul and began

speaking as soon as he answered. "We've got a problem. I'm aware you're in a meeting, but the Army is demanding more than the offer of ten percent discount on the missing shipment."

"Hmmm, playing hardball, are they? Is he some crotchety old military Chris?"

As irritated as she was at Captain Cartwright, hearing Saul speak of him in demeaning terms angered her.

"No, he's young, professional, and...well, to be honest...he has a point. They have to time their shipments out and this snafu cost them time and money. I feel as though we should offer more compensation."

"You're right, Evelyn. I'm sorry, that was an asinine comment. Look, I'll work up a proposal and email it to you in about five minutes. You can keep him busy for that long, can't you?"

"Sure." *Well, I'll let Molly do the entertaining.* "And thanks."

"No problem. Look, you're doing the right thing. It's just business. Always start out with a lowball offer and then you can go up."

Disconnecting, she leaned her back against the wall, while gently banging her head against the concrete. *I hate this part of the job. Three more months...surely I'll get the engineering job in three more months.* Sighing heavily, she jumped when her phone vibrated a few minutes later, indicating an incoming email. Looking at it, she smiled. *Good...this should work.*

Patrick's eyes looked from the bubbly Molly to Evelyn as she walked in. Her face appeared more relaxed and her body language more open. *'Bout time. Hopefully her boss decided to stop dickin' around.*

Molly smiled as she left and he turned his attention back to the woman seated again in front of him after she printed off several papers.

As she pushed them across the table, she smiled, saying, "I think you'll find this offer to be equitable for your time and trouble."

He looked down, impressed that he was now being offered a twenty percent refund on the missing ship- ment, a guarantee delivery date of Friday morning and a three percent discount on their next purchase with GMS, up to a certain price. Lifting his eyes, he nodded. "This is much more like it." Sending a message to his superior, he waited just a moment before receiving the okay to move forward.

"We have a deal," he said. "It's too bad your boss had to waste our time this morning."

The good feeling Evelyn had achieved disappeared with Patrick's last comment. *What a prick!* Plastering a smile on her face, she simply replied, "Fine. If you'll sign here, I'll have Molly print out the copies for you."

Seeing the narrowed eyes and glaring expression on her face, Patrick wondered what just happened. *Jesus, I just made a comment about her boss...not her.* Realizing the intrepid Ms. Sinclair seemed to be anxious to end the meeting, he just nodded.

Standing, Evelyn stuck her hand out one more time. "Then if you'll wait here, Molly will return shortly." She wanted to escape, but this time, the tingle from his hand to hers was impossible to ignore. Snatching her hand back quickly, she offered a curt nod before walking out of the room without a backward glance.

———————

Patrick watched Evelyn leave the room and rubbed his hand over his face. *Wow – way to fuck up a chance to get to know her!* He had been so shocked when he walked in and saw the woman from the pool. Considering he had jerked off in the shower twice with her on his mind since seeing her…*screwed that chance.*

Her boss set up her to fail at this meeting, he thought angrily. Sure, it was good business to lowball first then go up, but her boss would know that was not going to be acceptable. And Patrick had the feeling she had not been working there long enough to realize that. *And me getting pissed about it didn't help.*

Before he could process the events further, the bubbly Molly came back into the room with the papers for him to sign. She continued to babble as he tried to read over the contract. Finally, seeing everything in order, he signed and waited while she made copies.

"You must have really made an impression," Molly joked. "I've never seen Evelyn so flustered."

Sure that Molly's boss would be livid to know she was being discussed, Patrick was unable to stop asking more.

"Does she do this type of meeting often?"

"No, it's not her thing. She's an engineer and wanted a job in the plant, but," giving a little shrug, "she took the job working with military sales until an engineering job opened up for her." Scrunching her nose in thought, Molly continued, "She's got some super-duper engineering degree."

Why the hell would GMS put an engineer in this job? Unless they really wanted to hang on to her. Molly diverted his attention again as she handed him his copies.

"Thank you," he said as he packed his papers up to leave and then followed Molly out of the office. As they walked down the hall, he chanced a glance inside an office where the door stood open. There was Evelyn, standing in front of a tall filing cabinet, gently banging her head against the furniture as though she was trying to forget everything that had just happened.

Patrick grappled with the desire to rush in, pull her into his arms, and offer comfort while telling her she had done a good job with the negotiations. But she did not appear to want any company and he knew that would just embarrass her.

Turning, he followed Molly to the outside door, wishing the meeting could have been more amiable. *It doesn't matter,* he grumbled to himself. *I'll be leaving in a couple of months anyway. No time to start anything with the lovely Evie.* Climbing into his car, he pulled out of the parking lot, the image of her dark brown eyes in his mind. He acknowledged, *And she'd be no easy fuck. A woman like that...deserves it all.*

Saul stopped by Evelyn's office on Friday afternoon, seeing her sitting at her desk, typing away on her computer.

"Hey, I thought you'd be ready to head out for the weekend," he said, a perpetual grin on his face.

Looking up, she returned his smile. "For once, I don't want to work over the weekend, so I wanted to make sure I finished everything before I left."

He plopped down in a chair and shook his head. "Evelyn, you shouldn't work on the weekends. You need your down time."

"Oh, believe me, I utilize my down time," she said, leaning back. "But, sometimes, I feel like I need to take care of some things so I don't come in on Monday morning already behind."

"How did things end up with the Army shipment?" he asked.

"The Captain was a royal prick, but Saul, I felt stupid not knowing that the offer I made to him was a lowball offer."

He had the good grace to blush while ducking his head. "Sorry, Evelyn. That's just the way business is."

"Yes, but I don't have a business background!"

Nodding, he sat quietly for a moment before asking, "You still want a job in the plant?"

Stunned that he had to ask, she said, "Saul, you know I do. I find the sales part of the industry to be fascinating and it helps me understand how others use what we build, but my degree is in engineering."

"Well," he said, still smiling. "I just might have something that'll make your weekend better."

Afraid to hope, she cocked her head to the side. "Yeah?"

"It seems that one of the engineers will be retiring early...I've already talked to Gary and dad. They both say that you can have the job when he leaves, which should be in about a month."

The air left her lungs in a whoosh as she leaned forward, fist pumping the air. "Yes! Oh, my God, thank you!"

Laughing, Saul said, "Hey, this was always the agreement when you came on board with us. I'm just glad we can now work toward that." He sobered for a second before adding, "You do realize you would be working near Ed all day?"

Not even the idea of working with the surly, burly Ed could put a damper on her enthusiasm. "No worries! I can do this!"

"So, how about a celebratory drink after work?"

"Um, I've never been a drinker," she admitted. "But I'd love to celebrate."

"Sounds good. Follow me in your car and we'll go to a place near here. Not fancy, but good food and drinks."

Grinning at the turn of events, she shut down her computer and followed him outside. *Looks like things are finally going my way!*

5

Following Saul to the bar, Evelyn glanced nervously at her reflection in the rearview mirror, hoping she was not making a mistake. *This is not a date...just a celebratory drink...but I don't drink...so it's a celebratory...something. Jesus, I hope he doesn't get the wrong idea.* Before she could talk herself into heading home instead, she pulled into the parking lot behind him. It appeared, due to the number of cars—or rather jeeps, trucks, and SUVs— that the place was already hopping.

Getting out, she looked down at her attire and knew she was overdressed. Saul walked over and motioned for her to follow him. Hustling to catch up in her heels, she said, "Do you come here often?"

"I haven't been here for almost a year, but I swear they serve the best wings and I skipped lunch today." He halted just as they entered, giving them a chance to let their eyes adjust to the dim interior. There was a crowd, but they sighted a high-topped table near the front and he assisted her to her seat.

Once the waitress took their order, he looked at her, smiling like a little boy. "Look, Evelyn, here's the thing. I know you said you don't date co-workers and I respect that. So, I figured if I took you to some high-falutin' place for drinks, you'd feel self-conscious. But here? This is just a neighborhood bar with a bunch of people unwinding after a week of work. We're here as friends, okay?"

Smiling at his explanation, she nodded. "Perfect," she admitted.

A while later, a loud ruckus came from the back where a group of soldiers played pool. Twisting around to look behind her, she glanced through the crowd. Right in the middle of the group stood Captain Cartwright...staring straight at her.

Face flaming, she jerked her head toward Saul, choking on her food. Saul leaned over, slapping her on her back.

"You okay? The sauce go down wrong?" he yelled over the noise.

"Perhaps the lady needs some water," a familiar voice came from her side. Without turning, she recognized who it belonged to. *Perfect,* she thought. *My face is red, my eyes are watering, I have sauce on my cheeks, and Mr. Army Hunk walks over.* Grabbing her glass of water, she drank deeply, finally gaining control of herself.

Saul peered up at Patrick, a question in his eyes. Patrick stuck out his hand, introducing himself. "Captain Cartwright. Patrick. I met with Ms. Sinclair the other day."

Saul's eyes brightened with recognition. "Yes, yes.

Saul Oysten, here. I'm over the Financial Department of GMS. Glad everything worked out with the shipment replacement."

Evelyn watched as Patrick's eyes darkened, but before she could imagine why, he growled, "So you're the one who sent her in unprepared with that ridiculously low offer to begin with."

Saul shrugged, saying, "Business. Purely business. I assumed you wouldn't accept the first offer and we would come up to what was acceptable." Just then his phone buzzed and he glanced down at the message. Looking up apologetically, he said, "Evelyn, I'm sorry. I've got to head out. Dad's decided to convene a late meeting and needs me to come back."

She attempted to slide down from the high chair but found her way blocked by Patrick's large, immovable body.

"I'll see Evie's taken care of," Patrick said smoothly, and before she could object, Saul nodded, but a flash of jealousy crossed his expression. He appeared to want to say something, but shot her a tight smile instead, leaving the bar quickly.

Sliding into the seat vacated by Saul, Patrick looked over at the flushed...and visibly angry woman sitting across from him. *Looks like I've pissed her off again*, he thought ruefully, rubbing his hand along his jaw.

"Look, Evie," he began. "I'm not sure what I've done to make you so mad, but—"

"How about you just embarrassed me in front of my boss by implicating that I couldn't handle our meeting, for starters? Then you come over here, all caveman-like, to defend me? And now, you're sitting there like you... like you...I don't know. Like something!"

He opened his mouth to explain, but before he had a chance, she questioned, "And Evie? Evie? You don't know me and yet you've nicknamed me? Who does that?"

Patrick stared at her, words sticking in his throat. Today her hair was pulled back away from her face with a fancy clip, but the heavy length of glistening tresses hung over her shoulders, beckoning his fingers to discover if it was as soft as it looked. The simple makeup in place showcased her deep brown eyes and the mouth that he wanted to taste. Her lightweight sweater, in mint green, caressed perfect breasts and if he was any judge, they were natural. His eyes moved back to hers and he could not hold the grin from spreading across his face..

"Look, Evie. I was pissed the other day, but not at you. That guy," he indicated with a head jerk toward the door that Saul left from, "knew there was no way we would accept the low-ball offer and I got the distinct feeling that you didn't know that. It made you feel inadequate and awkward and I thought that was a shitty play on his part."

"I'm learning the business...at least in sales until I can move into the engineering job that's coming up," she answered back.

"So you're an engineer?" he asked, pretend surprise on his face.

Sighing deeply, Evie glared at him. "Why yes, Mr. Know-it-all. I'm sure it must be a shock to your system to realize that an intelligent woman might not be hideous at the same time!"

"Whoa," he exclaimed, putting his hands up in front of him. *Damn, I keep saying the wrong thing around her.* "I'm sorry. I didn't mean to be insulting about you being an engineer. I just meant that I was surprised an engineer was working in sales. That's all, I promise."

Blushing, Evie pulled her lips in, embarrassed to have misinterpreted his comment. "I'm sorry. Truly." She reached out and placed her hand on his, giving a slight squeeze before placing her hands back around her water bottle. "I have no idea why I'm lashing out at you. I suppose I find myself often having to defend my true vocation. There aren't a lot of women engineers in my field."

"I guess you get that kind of comment a lot, don't you?" he said, regret in his voice, already missing the touch of her hand on his. Deciding to change the subject, he asked, "So how's the investigation going?"

"Hmm?"

"The investigation...into where the missing partial shipment went?" he reiterated.

Her eyes darted down to her plate before moving back to his. "I don't actually know," she admitted. "I didn't ask any more after I was given the few cursory answers about the truck driver. It's not my job to search for it...if it really was missing."

"I assure you, it was missing," he said. "I understand that it's not your job...I'm just curious. Stealing equipment meant for our soldiers is a big business. Makes me fuckin' furious, but well...that's the way things are. I was just hoping that GMS had recovered it."

"Oh," she replied, embarrassed that she had never considered theft of military equipment. *No wonder he was pissed.* Before she could think of another comment, he continued.

"And the nickname…I don't know…I just think you look like an Evie," he shrugged, a playful grin on his face. "If you don't like it…" his voice trailed off.

Evie looked over at him, the wind suddenly going out of her sails. *How can a man look so devilishly handsome and like such a little boy all at the same time?* "No…it's…it's okay. I haven't been called Evie since I was much younger, so I guess it just took me by surprise, that's all. In college, all the professors used the full name, Evelyn, and then my employers do also."

"Surely your old friends and family still call you by Evie?" As soon as the words were out of his mouth he wanted to pull them back in, as he watched the light go from her eyes.

Faking a small smile, she slid from her stool and grabbed her purse. "It was…uh…nice to see you again, Captain Cartwright. I hope you have a nice evening with your friends." Turning, she was surprised to find his hand gently grasping her arm.

"I'm sorry if I said anything to offend you," he said, holding her gaze.

"No, no, it's fine. I'm tired and really need to go home." Pulling away, with a smile that did not reach her eyes, she weaved her way through the crowd and disappeared through the door.

What the fuck—

"Hey, man, did you strike out big time or what?" came the jovial question from Chris, who threw his arm around his friend.

Twisting his head around, Patrick admitted, "Damned if I know. I've seen the woman three times... three times I wanted to get to know her and three times I've been shut out."

"I'd say, three strikes, you're out buddy. Time to look for someone a little more accommodating." Chris carefully stared at his friend's face, a slow smile beginning. "Unless, of course...she's someone...special?"

"Fuck if I know what she is," Patrick answered before allowing himself to be pulled back to the pool tables.

———

Evie settled into the hot bath a few hours later, candles lit around the bathroom. Lying back, she sunk into the deep water until only her head appeared above the bubbles. Her mind ran over the events of the day, trying to focus on the upcoming engineering position she craved. Back to research... back to understanding how to make things stronger...how to build better machines and equipment. *People? I don't have a clue how to make them work.* As her muscles relaxed in the warmth, her mind drifted to the enigmatic Captain. *Patrick. The first man to call me Evie since my dad.* The thought of her father suddenly had her closing her eyes tightly, not wanting to allow the tears that stung the back of her eyes to escape.

If Patrick only knew...he'd never accuse me of trying to hide military thefts. After her skin had pruned, she stepped out of the tub and quickly donned her PJ shorts and a tank top. Shutting off the lights in her condo, she stopped and stared at the picture on the end table next to her sofa.

The smiling family faced the camera, their happiness evident in their expressions. Her father, in his military uniform, holding to her mother protectively, with Evie and Chrissie hanging on to both of them. Her dad had returned from an overseas tour in time to see her high school graduation. Who could have predicted he would not make it back from his next tour three years later?

Lying in bed, as the moon moved across the night sky, she realized she wanted to follow up on the missing shipment. *If there was a theft of military equipment from GMS, then I want to know about it!*

6

As the meeting came to a close, Norman asked if there was any other business that needed to be discussed. His expression was open and pleasant, but Evelyn hesitated for just a second, noticing the others around the table beginning to close their notebooks.

"Yes, I do," she announced, clearing her throat. As she realized all eyes had turned toward her, she continued. "I wanted to know what investigation was being conducted to find the missing materials...from the shipment to the Army Corps of Engineers base."

Norman appeared disconcerted for a moment and as her eyes moved around, she noted the expressions on the others' faces as well. Gary appeared uninterested, Saul's eyes darted nervously around the table, and Ed's normal glower darkened even more. The few others in attendance seemed surprised, as though they were unaware of what she was talking about.

"Evelyn," Gary began, "Ed talked to the truck driver who gave the statement that he missed a turnoff and was late getting there, did not know to sign the form, but according to him...all materials were delivered."

"Then how do we account for the missing items?" she continued.

"You ever consider the screw up wasn't on our end?" Ed growled.

Her gaze darted to his immediately. "Not on our end?"

Ed leaned forward menacingly, his meaty forearms resting on the table, and said, "Yeah. Not on our end. As in someone on the base miscounted...or got rid of what came in?"

"But...but...why would the military want to sabotage their own?"

"Jesus, how fuckin' naïve are you?" Ed bit out, leaning back heavily in his chair, causing it to squeak under his bulk.

"Ed!" Norman spoke sharply. "Language, please. This is still a business meeting. All may speak freely in here but keep your language professional."

Ed clamped his mouth shut, but his eyes glared daggers at Evelyn.

Gary continued, "It's our opinion that because the temporary truck driver did not follow procedures, we have no proof of any wrongdoing on his part and it is not uncommon for military personnel to sell some of their own equipment on the black market." Seeing Evelyn's eyes widen, he continued, "Black market sales are huge. They take a bite out of our profits and the military's ability to maintain their bases."

Evelyn's mind raced, never having considered that

the theft could occur on the base. Licking her lips as she pondered this idea, she noticed everyone was looking at her. Nodding slowly, she conceded, "I see your point. I think though that it would be nearly impossible for someone from the base to move the large transoms and side panels. It would take a truck to get them out of there."

"Evelyn, the inquiry is done," Saul said. "We've checked with the driver and we've taken the loss. You worked a nice deal with the military representative and now it's over. We won't be using that truck driver anymore and Ed has a checklist now prepared for each driver to go through when they make deliveries. Problem solved."

The air in the room grew thick as the assembly focused on her. Glancing toward Saul, she saw him offer her an encouraging smile. Clearing her throat again, she plastered a smile on her face. "All right, then. I suppose that's that."

The group smiled in relief and started moving from the room. Ed pushed by her in his normally rude manner, while Norman stopped her, saying, "I'm glad you asked, Evelyn. We don't want a habit of losing money or shipments." Patting her arm, he and Gary continued out into the hall.

Saul was the last to leave and he fell into step with her as they moved toward their offices. "Are you okay?" he asked.

Looking over at him, she shook her head. "Honestly? No. I hate the thought that someone from the Army base stole their own equipment..."

"But?" he prodded.

Twisting her head around to him as they approached her door, she said, "I don't believe they stole their own materials. I still think it was from this end and I can't believe no one wants to pursue the possibility more."

Neither spoke until they stopped at her office door. Looking up, she asked, "Is it hard, sometimes...working with your brother and dad?"

He glanced down the hall, then at his feet, before lifting his gaze back to hers. "Yeah, sometimes. Dad's the President, Gary's the Vice President. I got my finance degree and swore I'd never work for the family business. I wanted to be a success on my own, you know?" His eyes searched hers and seemed pleased when she offered a small nod. "But, there were a ton of people with business, finance, or accounting degrees when I got out, so, here I am."

He hesitated for a moment, then added, "Evelyn, don't get me wrong. I do well here, but sometimes...I wish I could get out from under their watchful eyes." Shrugging, he said, "But this is where I ended up."

Once more, the silence floated between them as Evie had no idea how to respond to his confession.

"If you want, I'll do some more digging? As head of Finance, I can ask questions easier than you can."

She smiled at him and nodded. "Yeah, I see where you could." Looking down the hall at the retreating backs of Gary and Norman, she said, "I'd like for you to check into it more. Just for our peace of mind."

Patrick walked out of Major Trumble's office and headed back to his own. His thoughts were jumbled, as he considered the Major's words. Patrick had been congratulated on his job performance and the Major asked him to consider re-upping for another tour. They discussed the missing equipment, the Major sure that the truck driver had delivered the partial load somewhere else for his own profit.

Sitting down heavily in his chair, he looked out of the window over the large equipment yard. His mind wandered to the beautiful Evie, wondering for the millionth time how she was doing. She looked so sad when she hurried out of the bar the week before.

Turning his thoughts from her, he watched as soldiers moved about the yard, his mind on the missing equipment. *No way this could have been from our end*, he surmised. *Not as big and heavy as the bridge parts are.* His mind always wanting to figure out a problem, he thought back to his grandfather. *Work it out, piece by piece. Like a puzzle. And then you can put it back together the right way.*

The more Patrick sat there, the more he wanted to know what had happened. *Investigating's not my job, but I sure as hell want to know.* Wondering how to get his hands on the internal report from GMS, he opened up his laptop. His fingers hesitated over the keys for a second, then plunged ahead. Typing an email to Evelyn, he requested an unofficial meeting. He erased and retyped the missive several times before it sounded the way he wanted—a mixture of personal and professional.

It was not long before he received his reply and to

his surprise, she agreed to meet with him at a local seafood restaurant. Smiling to himself, he typed out his gratitude. *Perfect...I get to see the woman that's filled my thoughts since I first saw her, and maybe can charm some information from her as well.*

The next evening, Patrick arrived at the restaurant early and had the hostess give him a corner table with lots of privacy and a view of the lake. He did not have to wait long before looking up and seeing the hostess escort Evie to him. Unable to hold back his smile, he stood as she approached.

Her rich hair was pulled back in its usual low ponytail and he itched to take it down, letting the strands caress her shoulders. Dressed in a rose-colored skirt that skimmed the tops of her knees and a cream-colored silk blouse, she appeared elegant... delectable. Her warm, brown eyes met his and she ducked her head as a slight blush appeared on her cheeks. *Interesting...she's a fighter...and shy.* Thinking of that combination in his bed had him grabbing her hand and ushering her into her seat so that he could sit as well to hide his growing erection. *Fuck, man. Get a grip!*

"I was surprised to get your email," she said, cocking her head to the side. "You wanted to talk?"

"Yes, but first, let's order." As the waitress came over to them, he ordered a beer and then added, "And for the lady, a glass of Voss Sparkling."

Her eyes widened as she looked at him. "How did you—"

"I remembered you only drank water at the bar, so I assumed you didn't drink alcohol," he admitted, his face suddenly uncertain as he queried, "Was I right?"

She smiled at his sudden little boy expression again. "Yes, you are. Thank you." She nervously fiddled with her napkin, placing it in her lap, keeping her eyes from the blue, piercing ones sitting across from her. When she had opened her email, seeing his request for an informal meeting, she had no idea if it were a date, a business meeting, or something in between. And curiosity had gotten the better of her. *Admit it, girl... you're interested...even if he's off limits!*

The silence overtook and she lifted her eyes to his, seeing the sparkle in their blue depths. The blue dress shirt he wore stretched over his muscular body. He appeared casual...*and deadly gorgeous*. His hair, military short, showcased his features to perfection. His intelligent eyes, square jaw, and beautiful lips turned up in a smile. Jerking herself out of her musings, she said quickly, "Um, so what did you want to talk about?"

"Evie...uh, is Evie all right?" he asked, realizing the use of her nickname might not be a good place to start building something if the name made her prickly again.

"Yes, Evie is fine," she admitted, a slow smile curving the corners of her mouth.

"I'm glad. I didn't want to upset you again."

Looking down for a moment, she shook her head. "No, no. Really, it's fine. My father always called me Evie."

He stayed silent, hoping she would continue to speak. She did not disappoint.

"My father was in the Army," she said, fiddling with her napkin before lifting her gaze back to his, seeing Patrick's eyes widen in surprise. "We traveled a lot... growing up. Different bases, different schools."

"I take it you didn't like that very much?"

Smiling wistfully, she confessed, "No, I didn't. My older sister was outgoing and loved to travel. She made friends wherever we landed. Me? Not so much. I was the geeky, smart girl who was shy. I vowed when I finally grew up, I would find a place to live and stay put forever."

Patrick thought about telling her his plans to move to Virginia in a few months but found the words choking in his throat. *No need to bring that up now,* he told himself.

"Anyway," she continued with a delicate shrug, "my family always called me Evie. Once an adult, everyone called me Evelyn. The name seemed more professional and so I just stuck with it."

"Where's your dad stationed now, or did he retire?" The dark shadow passed through her eyes again and he realized his blunder too late. "Oh, Evie, I'm so—"

"No, it's all right," she reassured him. "Well, it's not all right, but it is what it is. Dad didn't come back after his last tour. He was killed in Iraq six years ago."

"Fuck, Evie," he said, "I had no idea I was bringing up something like this for you." He reached across the table, taking her hand in his.

She felt the warmth of his fingers caressing hers for

a moment then smiled. "We were stationed in California last and so that's where I stayed. My sister got married out of college and now lives in North Carolina where her husband is from. Mom moved there to be close to her grandchildren. We miss dad terribly...but as mom says, he would have wanted us to keep living. So we do...with his memory always close."

The two sat in comfortable silence for a few minutes, his hand still holding hers, gently rubbing her fingers.

"So, enough about me," she concluded, finally pulling her fingers back. "What did you want to meet about?"

Patrick leaned back in his seat, staring at the enigmatic woman sitting across from him and rethought his position. He came to charm her into giving him information but that deceit died quickly in him. *Ah, hell. Just go with the truth and if she leaves...fuck, I'll just have to accept it.*

"To be truthful, I wanted to ask you about the report. The one that your company would have completed, when the shipment went missing. I can't get the missing equipment out of my head and considered doing a little investigating on my end." He held his breath for a moment, wondering if she would storm out in anger.

Eyes widening, she exclaimed, "You too? I've been thinking the same thing."

Releasing his breath in relief, he said, "Do you think that you could share your report with me?"

Her face scrunched in thought before she said, "I'm not sure if it's public or not."

"Evie, I'm fairly certain that it's not." He let the

words hang out in the air between them, giving her a chance to discern his meaning.

Suddenly, she jerked back, her eyes piercing his. "You're asking me to give you information that you don't really have a right to, aren't you? Patrick, I could lose my job! And how do you know it wasn't on your end?"

"I don't," he replied honestly. "But the odds of someone being able to transfer the large, heavy equipment off base once it was there is minimal."

She sighed long and slowly, admitting, "I know. I already thought of that when I brought the missing shipment back up in a meeting."

So, she's been thinking of this also...enough to talk to her superiors about it. "How'd that go for you?"

Grimacing, she said, "Not very well. Everyone considers the inquiry closed. Well, except for Saul. He's the man who was with me the other night."

A flash of jealousy bolted through Patrick as he attempted to tamp down those unfamiliar feelings. "Is he your...?"

"Oh, my goodness, no! I don't date in the workplace," she exclaimed. Blushing, she admitted, "And he's...well, he's just a friend."

A friend who wants in your pants, Patrick thought with irritation. "You sure he feels that way?"

"I've let him know," she answered, then her lips thinned before adding, "Why am I telling you this? My personal life is none of your business."

"If we're going to be working together, I think it's my business if this guy could be a complication."

"Working together? Who says we're working together?" Evie defended.

"Look, Evie. You and I both want to discover what happened. We want the truth. And since the military and your company are moving forward without getting answers, you and I should put our heads together and solve the puzzle. We're both engineers...call it our nature to solve puzzles."

She settled back in her seat as their food was delivered. For a few minutes, neither spoke, each enjoying their food and pretending the elephant was not sitting at the table with them.

Finally sighing, she said, "You're right. I want to know the truth. I hate the idea of someone stealing military equipment. How do I know my dad might not have been killed if all his equipment was with him? And the soldiers now...they need what you requisition for them."

Nodding his agreement, Patrick reached back across the table to grasp her hand but, before he could say anything, she continued. "And we need to set some ground rules. This is professional only." Blushing, she rushed on, "Not that you meant this to be anything else, but I wanted to put that out there."

Grinning, he squeezed her hand. "We'll see, Evie. For now...just professional. But who knows what we'll build."

Biting her lip, she nodded, uncertainty filling her expression. *But can I tell my heart that? I could so easily fall for him...and then he'd be assigned somewhere else...and I'd be left behind.*

7

As Patrick walked Evie back to her car, he kicked himself for not offering to pick her up so that they could spend more time together. Turning to her as they stopped by her driver's door, he said, "We need to get together soon...to go over what we think may have happened."

She lifted her gaze to his, nodding her agreement. "I'll see what I can get my hands on tomorrow and then maybe..."

"Tomorrow's perfect," he rushed. "I could come over. I'll even bring Chinese."

"Now, who can resist that?" she laughed, noticing his dimples for the first time. "I live in the—"

"I know where you live," he admitted, his eyes twinkling. "I happened to be there a few weeks ago and noticed you by the pool."

Blushing, she said, "Oh...uh...oh."

"Don't worry," he replied, lifting his hand to smooth a strand of hair back behind her ear. "I don't think you even noticed me." He watched as the setting sun sent shimmers through her hair as a few more strands blew free from her ponytail.

"I did," she acknowledged. Heaving a sigh, she confessed, "It would be hard not to notice you. But then I saw your military dog tags around you neck and...uh..."

"And the last thing you wanted to do was be around someone in the military. Too many memories...I get it."

Placing her hand on his muscular arm, she hurried to explain. "That seems so judgmental, hearing it from you. I'm sorry."

"Don't be," he said, stepping closer to her, battling between wanting to press her body between his tall frame and her car. "Would it make a difference if I told you that I will be discharged in less than three months?"

Her eyes widened, moving back and forth between his. "Really?"

Smiling, he nodded. "Yep, so you can become my... sleuthing partner, without fear of me going back overseas."

Grinning in return, she thrust out her hand and replied, "Agreed, partner."

Taking her hand in his, he lifted it to his lips instead of shaking it. "Until tomorrow." Placing a soft kiss on her fingers, he assisted as she slid into the driver's seat of her car and stood to watch as she drove away.

You didn't tell her you were moving back to Virginia in three months, asshole, he chastised himself. Giving a mental shake, he thought, *it doesn't matter. I need her help to find out where the missing items are and once we do, perhaps...well, perhaps...* Frustrated, he hauled his long frame up into his Jeep and drove home.

The next day, Evie downloaded the report and printed it. She had read through it but had not paid close attention to the statement from the substitute truck driver. It was only two printed lines, giving no more detail than what she had read before. But it had his name. She tried to google his name and address but did not come up with anything. Since that was the extent of her investigative skills, she shoved the printed copies into her oversized purse. Not wanting to use company email, she sent Patrick a text telling him what she had.

He sent one in return, asking for the name. After typing it to him, she startled when Saul poked his head into her office.

"Whoa, sorry to scare you," he said, laughing as he walked in.

"Oh, I must have been daydreaming," she replied, pushing her phone down in her lap. "What can I do for you?" she asked, her voice more curt than she intended.

"Well," he said, "I didn't think it was a bad thing for me to just come over and visit. But if you're busy..."

"No, no, I'm just distracted."

"Thinking about the new job?"

Smiling, she admitted, "Yes. I've talked to Human Resources and, of course, I have to reapply, which I actually did this morning."

"Yeah, but you realize that's just a formality?"

"I hope so. I understand when GMS hired me, I was told that I would be up for the next engineering position, but you know how things can get screwed up."

"Listen, Evelyn, I know you and I spoke about trying to find out more about what happened to that shipment and I was all ready to help you...and I still am," he rushed on, "but, well maybe this isn't the right time."

Cocking her head to the side, she was curious. It had been in her mind to ask him to help her and Patrick, but now she needed to hear what he had to say.

"It's just that I overheard dad and Gary talking yesterday. They want to avoid any negative publicity. If there was something that happened, they want it handled in-house." Rubbing his hand over his face, he looked up at her. "I'd like to help...I've just never been very good about going against what they wanted."

She saw his dejected face and realized that before talking to Patrick, she would have felt sorry for Saul, but right now...all she felt was irritation. *If there's something going on, then it needs to stop, not be swept under the rug.* Another realization slammed into her at the same time. *I was attracted to Saul at one time...but now, seeing him after spending just a little time with Patrick...No comparison! I'm glad I put Saul firmly into the friendship-only zone.*

Patrick placed a call and before he heard his sister's voice, he could hear the squeals of little girls in the background. *She must be catering another party.* After a few seconds, Angel had moved to a quieter location and greeted her brother enthusiastically.

"Are you calling to tell me you're moving here early?"

Chuckling, he replied, "No, no. The Army'll keep me until the end." They chatted a few more minutes about family and friends and then he said, "Listen, I'm checking into something here and I'd like to be able to get the Saints to help out a little. Could you give me Monty's phone number?"

"Sure," she said, rattling it off. "Does this mean you're thinking about working for Jack when you move here?"

"Let's not get ahead of ourselves, Sis. Anyway, I'll let you get back to the princess party. Talk to you soon."

Disconnecting, he placed the call to Monty Lytton, Angel's fiancé, who worked for an elite company, the Saints Protection & Investigations. After greetings and a few minutes of pleasantries, he got down to business.

"I need some help and thought I'd reach out to you first to see what you thought." It took several minutes to bring Monty up to speed on the missing equipment. "So, the problem is that I have an inquisitive mind but not the tools to figure things out."

"Tell you what, Patrick," Monty said. "Give me the name of the driver and I'll have our computer guru, Luke, check on things for you. I'll also talk to Jack and see what we can work out." Chuckling, he added, "Does this mean you're thinking of joining the Saints when you move to Virginia?"

"Angel asked the same thing. I honestly don't know

right now what I want to do, but let me finish my Army job and work on the investigation of this missing equipment. Then we'll talk."

"Sounds good," Monty replied. "I'll call you with what Luke finds."

After the call, Patrick sat in his chair for a while, staring out of the window once more. The Army had been good to him, but after his last tour of duty, he no longer felt the desire to return to a war zone. Sitting at the desk job had solidified his resolve to not re-up again, even if he stayed stateside. He watched as soldiers used forklifts to move the materials around to get them loaded for transport. The idea of finding out exactly what happened to the missing equipment fired through him.

His phone vibrated with an incoming message from Monty. **Driver – Chris Tompkins. Addrs – 114 Carbo St., Sacr.**

Jesus, Luke works fast. The idea of being able to investigate with the right tools at his fingertips sounded better and better each day. Remembering what he learned when he visited his sister a few months ago, he knew the company was started by Jack Bryant, a former Army Special Forces Chief Warrant Officer. Jack had the opportunity to work with a diverse group of men on several critical missions and when he was honorably discharged, he replicated that in the civilian world. Monty had been former FBI. He knew Luke was former CIA. Patrick did not know the rest of the group, other than hearing some were from DEA, police, ATF, and probably other members of the government alphabet soup.

What they would all bring to the table...fuckin' hell...an investigator's dream team. Maybe, just maybe, that's for me.

Another vibration from his phone jerked him back to the present. A second text came in from Monty. **Jack says he's on board. Keep us informed.**

Patrick's grin slashed across his face. *I may be on the other side of the country, but looks like I'm working with some Saints!*

Evie nervously paced her condo waiting on Patrick. She had changed into comfortable yoga pants and a long, tunic blouse that hung below her ass. He said he would bring the food, but she had beer for him and tea for herself, plus she indulged and purchased cheesecake from a bakery down the road.

Walking by the mirror once more, she debated pulling her hair up, when there was a knock on the door. Throwing it open, she stood dumbfounded as she looked at the man standing on her stoop. A tight black t-shirt pulled over the muscles she remembered distinctly. Faded jeans, faded in all the right places. Long toes sticking out of flip-flops. Staring at his feet, she wondered, *How the hell are toes sexy?* But they were and held her attention. Hearing him clear his voice, her head jerked up, a blush blazing across her face.

"Oh, um...come in," she stammered.

Grinning, he entered her apartment accompanied by

the delectable scent emanating from the bags in his hands. While she had been perusing him, his eyes had taken a trip themselves.

He had seen her in professional attire, supporting his knowledge that she was beautiful. He had seen her in a bathing suit, supporting his knowledge that she was gorgeous. But seeing her almost makeup free, shining face, hair hanging down about her shoulders, and comfortable clothing that, while modest, did nothing to hide her curves... he wanted to drop to the floor and worship her. Discreetly moving the bags to the front, he hid his hard-on while giving his dick a stern talking-to. *Don't embarrass me now...the last thing I want to do is scare her off!*

They sat down to sesame shrimp, chicken fried rice, cheese rangoons, and egg rolls. Moaning orgasmically, Evie loved every bite, unknowingly causing Patrick to shift several times to ease his erection. Conversation over dinner was easy, mostly about their engineering degrees.

"Remember how many girls were in your engineering classes?" she asked.

He thought back, but admitted, "Not really, there were so few."

"Yep," she nodded. "I loved what I was learning but it was a lonely major for a woman. The other engineering students didn't want to date me, especially if I performed better than they did on a project. I studied all of the time, so I never went to frat parties. And as soon as I would meet a guy, once I told him I was in the

Geomaterials Engineering program...his eyes would glaze over and he'd beat a path to the door."

"I guess on top of moving around from base to base as a child, you did feel isolated," he acknowledged, understanding more than ever her desire to find a home where she felt as though she belonged.

"That's why I made a vow to stay put. I've got a good job and I'll soon be hired with GMS as an engineer. I've got this great condo," she continued, waving her chopstick around. "And I'm not moving again!"

Patrick shifted uncomfortably in his chair again, this time not to ease his erection, but out of guilt. *I should tell her I'm moving in a couple of months. To the other side of the country. Fuck!*

He glanced around the condo and saw comfortable furniture—the kind you buy when you land your first big job and want to finally spend some money to make a home. She had knick-knacks around, candles, cute lamps, and family pictures. *She's turned this place into a home...a real home.*

"So tell me about you?" she asked, spearing another piece of shrimp.

"I always loved to tinker...puttered around with my granddad as a kid. He was proud when I became an engineer, even prouder when I joined the Army, and about busted his buttons when he came to my Special Forces graduation. I was the Company Executive Officer and helped train the Special Forces Engineer Sergeants. Did two tours in Afghanistan and decided that was it for me. Loved the military, but was ready to move to the next phase of my life."

Scrunching her nose, she cocked her head and asked, "So how'd you end up in California?"

"To finish out my time in service, I was assigned to the Corps of Engineers base here. It gives me a chance to oversee the equipment requisitions that we used in the field."

"What's next for you...besides investigating skullduggery?"

"Skullduggery?" he questioned, laughing while choking on a bite of egg roll. Coughing, he tried to appear suave while trying not to sputter, but knew he was failing miserably.

Evie jumped up and began slapping him on his back, only to make the coughing worse. Twisting, she grabbed her glass of tea and assisted him to take a few sips. "I'm so sorry!" she exclaimed.

As he recuperated, he grinned. *Skullduggery? What a goof!* "It's all good," he assured. "You just caught me off guard." Catching her hand in his as she moved to sit back down, he squeezed it. "You're a breath of fresh air, Evie."

Blushing, she moved back to her seat, picking up her chopsticks again before looking at him, waiting for his answer.

"I haven't made any firm commitments for after I get out. I could use my civil engineering degree and work for a company...or who knows," he admitted evasively.

Nodding, she accepted his answer and looked down at the mostly empty containers. "So where do we want to start?" she asked, gathering the plates from the table. Putting everything away, she turned back and said, "Let's sit in the living room and see what we've got."

Wanting to keep her interested in him, he kept his mouth shut about the move. *We're just working together right now. Nothing more. I don't need to tell her my long-range plans.* The more he tried to convince himself that they could keep everything professional, the more he knew it was a lie.

They sat on opposite ends of the sofa, facing each other. She set her tea on the coffee table next to his beer, before turning her attention back to him. He watched her carefully, loving the way her face was so expressive. No pretense. Just honest emotion.

He began, "I talked to my sister's fiancé and he got the address of the truck driver. I was going to go see him tomorrow after work—"

"I want to come also," Evie exclaimed excitedly.

Looking askance, Patrick said, "I don't think that's a good idea."

"Oh please! It'll be broad daylight and we'll talk to him on his stoop. What harm can come from that?"

As much as he hated the thought of her being involved, he had to admit that she might have insight when talking to the driver.

Taking a sip of her tea, she looked at him as he appeared to be puzzling over something. "So what do you think happened?"

Leaning back on the sofa, he said, "The easiest explanation is that the driver went somewhere and had someone arrange to take the equipment off of the truck. Then he drove to the base with what was left."

"But that would have taken organization...time to plan. He was a substitute truck driver, not the regular one. How would he even know when he was being called?" she asked.

Patrick wrestled with how much he should tell her about his fears, but understood she was smart enough to begin putting all the puzzle pieces together by herself. Sighing, he plunged ahead, "Then that would indicate that someone from the inside knew what was going to happen, when it was going to happen, make the arrangement...including needing the truck driver."

Evie's eyes opened wide at the implication. *Someone from the inside? Inside of my workplace? Maybe someone I know?*

8

Patrick saw the look of distress cross Evie's face and was filled with the desire to take it away. "We don't know...we don't know it was someone you might work with. It might have been some arrangement the truck drivers made."

Nodding hesitantly, she searched his eyes. "But it could be, couldn't it? It could be someone inside GMS... someone I know...someone I work with."

"Damn, Evie, I'm not sure," he sighed heavily, leaning back against the sofa. Keeping his gaze on hers, he watched as her mind began to puzzle through possibilities. *Sharp as a fuckin' tack. She'll be questioning everyone she meets at GMS.* "Look, we have to play this cool. The last thing we want is someone getting spooked because you're asking a lot of questions and snooping around."

Disgust crossed her face as she scowled. "I'm not that naïve! I'm not going to go into work and announce 'Hey y'all, who was involved in stealing equipment?'"

"Down, tiger. I didn't mean to imply that you would

do that." He grinned, then gave in to the desire to lean over and gently brush a strand of hair back behind her ear. The fire remained in her eyes, but he knew the instant it changed from irritation to lust. Moving ever so slowly toward her, he halted a whisper away from her lips. His gaze, speaking his question, received the answer he longed for and he leaned in further. His lips met hers, in a barely-there kiss...almost more of a touch than a taste.

Leaning back, his gaze continued to search hers, this time seeing a thread of doubt mixed with the lust. *Don't do this, man. Don't cross this line.* His head attempted to rule his heart, but the pounding of his blood drowned out the voice. Angling his head, he claimed her lips, moving over them, tasting them, memorizing them. Licking her seam, he plunged when they opened beneath his.

Pulling her body closer to his, he settled her on his lap, her back against his left arm and her legs now stretched out across the sofa cushions. Cupping her jaw with his right hand, he smoothed his rough thumb over her silken cheek. He only meant the kiss to satisfy his curiosity, assuage his need for her, but it flamed and he had no desire to douse the fire.

Evie, her chest heaving as his lips continued their assault on her senses, clung to his shoulders for balance. Giving into the moment, her tongue sucked on his, swallowing his groan.

Twisting their heads back and forth, noses bumping, tongues tangling, both lost to the lust rolling through their veins. Long, wet kisses consumed them as their hands grasped each other closely. The words of his grandfather resounded in his ears, pushing out the roar. *Gotta build it right, make sure the parts fit together, protect it...Damn.* He knew they could build something; knew they fit together, but he was not protecting her heart by lying to her.

As though in agony, Patrick pulled back, her mewl of discontent almost causing him to move right back in, continuing to kiss her until he knew he would flip her underneath him, taking her body the way he had imagined ever since seeing her at the pool.

His hands held her face in place as she attempted to move back in closer. "I...we...we can't, Evie," he panted. Pulling away from her took all his willpower, his hands shaking as they held her shoulders back away from him.

Evie, jolted from her lust-induced fantasy, looked askance as she realized her body was fighting to move back into his. Her hand touched her lips, still tingling from his assault. Blushing furiously, she attempted to jump off his lap. "I'm sorry, I—"

"No, no, babe, don't you dare say you're sorry," he demanded, holding her in place. Lifting her chin with two of his fingers, he held her gaze. "You've got nothing to be sorry about. This was me...all me...and as much as I want you, I don't want to fuck this up."

A questioning expression crossed her face as she peered back at him. "Fuck what up, Patrick?"

"This...us...what we feel and what we're building here."

Shaking her head, silently expressing her misunder-
standing, she waited as he pulled his thoughts together.
He gently moved her off his lap and stood, beginning to
pace her living room.

"Shit, fuck, Evie," he said, stopping in front of the
garden doors leading out to her deck, staring out into
the night sky. Turning around, he saw her confused
expression, doubt in her eyes. Stalking back over, he
dropped to his knees, crouching in front of her, clasping
her hands in his. "I'm sorry. I can't lead you on like this.
I gotta come clean."

Sighing heavily, he continued, "Almost everything
I've told you is the truth…I'm getting out of the Army in
a couple of months, I'm dedicated to finding out what
happened to that missing equipment, and I want to
work with you to do that. But I can't come in here and
just charm the information out of you." Licking his lips,
he cupped her jaw. "I like you, Evie. I liked what I saw
when you were out by the pool, then respected the
woman I met in our first meeting. Everything about you
makes me want to get to know you better…see if we
fit…see if we can build something."

She breathed in every word he said, cheering at the
honesty, discovering he was as interested in her as she
was in him…*but something's holding him back.* Remaining
quiet, she waited to see what was coming.

"The only thing I wasn't honest about was what
I'm doing when I get out." His eyes darted back and
forth between hers, searching for any reaction,
finding none…other than caution. Sucking in a deep
breath, he said, "My sister and her fiancé live in

Virginia. So do my parents...when they aren't vacationing in Florida." He hesitated, seeing his explanation slowly dawn on her before he continued. "I...I've decided to move back to Virginia. I'm not certain what I'll be doing there, but I want to be closer to family. My sister's getting married and I want to be around her."

Nodding in a way that seemed more expected than real, she silently glanced over his shoulder at the framed family photograph on her wall. Her dad, in his military uniform, with his arm proudly around her mom's shoulders, Evie and her sister standing in front of them. Her dad's other hand rested on her, pulling her gently back into his strength. The family was smiling...a real smile from something amusing and not fake from a photographer's insistence. *He wants to be closer to his family.*

"Evie?" he whispered.

Her eyes jerked back to his, nodding this time with more emotion. "Thank you...for um...well, thank you for being honest with me."

"You're upset?"

She watched the myriad of expressions cross his face. *Concern. Guilt. Hope.* Reaching out, she moved to cup his face before her fingers halted. "I have no right to be upset," she said. "I...well, thank you." Slipping away from him, she stood and moved to the kitchen. "Do you want another beer while we finish planning?"

Patrick dropped his chin to his chest, his heart heavy. He knew she was smart. *No sense in trying to build something that'll just end in a couple of months anyway.*

Heaving another huge sigh, he stood following her. "Sure, that'd be great."

Lying in bed that night, Evie relived the evening's ending.

Separating from the sofa, they danced around each other, pretending the kiss of all kisses had not happened. They continued to discuss the problem and decided to talk with the truck driver that weekend. Patrick had shown concern about her going but she had been insistent. "I'll make him feel less threatened," she had claimed and in the end, Patrick agreed.

They also talked about the people she came in contact with on a daily basis at GMS, but it seemed that her range of contacts was minimal. "I'll keep my ears and eyes open," she promised and as he walked to the door, they stood awkwardly saying goodbye.

Finally, he nodded sadly as she stepped back and closed the door.

Now, hours later, she still could not sleep. Rolling over, she punched her pillow, huffing in frustration. Knowing sleep was not coming, she climbed out of bed, padding into the kitchen to make a cup of herbal tea. Once it steeped, she moved to the garden doors, stepping out onto her small deck overlooking the park near the back of the property.

Settling in one of the lounge chairs, she pulled her robe tighter around her, blocking out the spring coolness, and sipped her tea.

What's really bothering me? The fact that I was falling for him, and now he's beyond my reach? At least he was honest, telling me the truth before we went too far. Her mind wrestled with the swirl of emotions, all vying for attention.

Patrick leaving in a couple of months to the other side of the country. Norman and Gary dismissing the possible theft, not wanting negative publicity. Saul, saying they were friends but seeming to want more. The new engineering job that would be hers in a couple of weeks.

Leaning back, she lifted her eyes toward the stars, feeling alone. Bone-wearyingly alone. Her mind drifted back the picture of her family and a small smile escaped amidst the turmoil. *I'm sorry dad. I never meant to imply that your Army career was bad...or not enough. I just hated moving, that's all. It wasn't easy for me to make friends.* Sighing deeply as she sipped the last of her tea, she felt her father's presence as though his arms wrapped around her. *I want what you and mom had, dad. I want to wake up every morning, so happy to be beside the man in bed with me. I want him to look at me the way you looked at mom.*

She leaned over, setting the mug on the table and walked to the railing, looking out over the peaceful night. *Maybe...if I had that...I would not be so afraid to step out of my comfort zone.* Walking inside, she set her mug in the sink and made her way back to bed. Sliding under her covers once more, she felt sleep begin to take her over the edge. *What could we have built together, Patrick?* she wondered, slipping into a deep sleep.

Miles away, in the pre-dawn morning, the sound of Patrick's feet pounded a rhythm along the American River at Sutter's Landing Park. Unable to sleep, he finally decided to sweat out the frustration coursing through his body.

After ending the kiss that rocked him to his soul, they continued to discuss the case as though the clench of the century had not just happened. Rounding a curve he slowed his pace, taking in the rising sun over the water. *Fuck! Why now? Why when I'm leaving, do I have to find someone I could see forever in her eyes?*

Walking for another mile, his mind turned once more toward his grandfather. *Just because parts don't fit, don't mean they weren't good parts. Sometimes when you're building somethin', things just don't go together.*

Making his way to his jeep in the parking lot, he climbed in and began the drive back to his apartment. Several minutes later, stepping into the hot shower, washing off the sweat, his mind continued to focus on Evie.

Damn, Granddad...I think these parts coulda fit together perfectly. Maybe I just need to work on them a little more. With that thought giving him hope, he dressed proudly in his uniform, ready to face the challenges of a new day with renewed vigor.

9

Saturday morning, Patrick pulled up outside Evie's condo and watched as she bounded down the steps toward his jeep. Dressed in jeans that fit her curves perfectly and a lightweight green sweater, her thick hair was pulled back with a headband and curled about her shoulders.

Hopping out, he jogged around the front, opening the door for her. "Your chariot awaits, m'lady," he said, offering her a hand up.

Placing her hand over her heart, she cooed, "Oh, thank you!"

Once on their way to the address of the errant driver, their conversation became more stilted. Looking sideways, Patrick asked, "Are you nervous?"

"Yeah," she confessed. "To be honest, I am."

He reached across the console, taking her cold fingers and linking his with hers, offering a squeeze of comfort. "It'll be fine," he promised. "We're just going to ask some questions and not be threatening."

Glancing at the large man holding her hand, she lifted her eyebrows. "Seriously? As big as you are, you don't think you'll be threatening?"

Chuckling, he said, "Well, that's why I agreed to let you come with me. You're supposed to mitigate the threat, right?"

Grinning, she settled back and tried to still the knots in her stomach. Too soon, they pulled in front of a small, older house. A tricycle and bicycle littered the otherwise neat lawn, and a man, tinkering with a lawn-mower, squatted in the driveway.

Parking in the street in front of the house, Patrick hopped out, walked around, and assisted Evie down from his Jeep.

The man stood as the two approached him, a questioning expression on his face. "Can I help you?"

"I hope so," Patrick replied affably. "I'm Captain Cartwright of the Army Corps of Engineers and this is Ms. Sinclair from GMS." He noted the man's eyes sharpened as he looked between the two. "We're looking for Chris Tompkins and wanted to ask a few questions about the shipment that was delivered to the base."

Scowling, Chris grumbled, "I already made a statement about that."

Before Patrick replied, Evie spoke up. "I know and I did read your report." Leaning in conspiratorially, she said, "But we're checking to see who might have taken the equipment...you know..." she jerked her head toward Patrick.

Chris' expression changed as he said, "You think it was someone from inside the base?"

Patrick wanted to punch something but wisely kept his mouth shut. Evie gave a noncommittal shrug and it seemed to work. Chris' expression relaxed and his demeanor became less blustery.

"Maybe we could sit on your porch in the shade and talk for a few minutes," she suggested sweetly.

Chris glanced back at his house and then nodded. "Yeah, come on up." Once there, he leaned his head inside and yelled, "Babe, got some business to take care of out here. Can you bring some coffee?"

The three sat on the porch chairs and from outward appearances looked to be a gathering of friends. A few minutes later, a small, dark-haired woman appeared with three mugs of coffee, her eyes moving curiously between Patrick and Evie. Two children popped outside also, staring at the visitors. Mrs. Tompkins shooed the children inside and then disappeared back into the house also, after resting her hand momentarily on her husband's shoulder.

Evie noted the gesture and prayed that Chris had not been involved in the theft, realizing the ramifications would be devastating to the family.

"Whatcha need to know?" Chris asked.

"Basically, could you just walk us through the whole process, from the time you were contacted to the time you finished the delivery?" Patrick requested.

Taking a long sip of his coffee, Chris nodded slowly but kept his eyes down on his mug. "I'm just a substitute truck driver for GMS. I normally drive for the Driveways Sealant Company, here in town. They usually keep me pretty busy, but occasionally on a day off from them, I can pick up extra work as a sub. GMS isn't the only company I sub for, but I've been used by them more 'an once."

Taking another long sip, he continued. "Got a call one morning asking if I'd be able to do a large load run that day. 'Course I said yeah, 'cause the money's always good with GMS."

"Who called you?" Patrick asked.

"Same as always," Chris replied. "Man named Ed. He's the plant manager or somethin' like that."

Ed? Evie almost choked on her coffee but knew that Ed would have been the one to call. Her stomach twisted again, the coffee now tasting bitter. *Why did it not dawn on me that I'd possibly be hearing things I'd rather not hear?*

"Okay, go on, please," Patrick encouraged, his eyes jerking to Evie's. Offering her a questioning gaze, he nodded when she gave a halfhearted smile.

Chris leaned back in his chair and rubbed his hand over his face, exuding frustration. Sighing heavily, he finally leveled his gaze toward Patrick and said, "I didn't do nothin' wrong. Swear to God, I wish now I'd never answered the fuckin' phone. Because of the mess, I won't be gettin' any more business from GMS and that's fine by me. It's less money, but I'm sticking to the Driveway's business and not messing around with sub work."

"What happened, Chris?" Evie asked, her voice soft and encouraging.

"By the time I got to GMS, the other trucks were already gone. I just signed off on whatever paperwork was put in front of me and that's not uncommon. I'm not there when the shit...uh, sorry ma'am...when the stuff is loaded into the trucks. I was given the directions but they'd been programmed into the GPS that was in the truck cab. So I just climbed in, and started driving."

"What time was this?" Patrick asked.

"'Bout nine-thirty in the morning. The other trucks had long since gone."

Patrick knew the other trucks had left GMS at almost eight o'clock and had made their deliveries by nine-thirty. This would have left Chris completely on his own with the delivery.

"I followed the directions and ended up at some warehouse near the docks. I got out and talked to a couple of the men who were standing around. They invited me inside so I could check my directions and, honestly," he looked embarrassed, "I needed a pis...um, needed to use the restroom. I swear I was only inside for probably about twenty minutes. I used the men's room, went to an office and called GMS back to check on the address. I was told they screwed up and gave me the wrong one. They gave me the correct delivery location and I headed back out."

"Did you notice anything different about the truck? Doors open, truck moved...anything?" Patrick prodded.

Shaking his head, Chris confirmed, "Nope. Keys were still in the ignition, truck still where I left it."

"Chris, could anyone have gotten inside and taken

some of the equipment while you were inside the building?" Evie queried.

Sighing heavily, Chris drained his mugful of coffee. He nodded slowly and admitted, as he ticked off points on his fingers, "Yeah, I guess. But they'd have to have known I was coming and had men and forklifts ready. They'd have to have known what was in the truck and they'd have to have worked fast." He looked up at them and said, "It's possible, but damn, it would have to be organized."

Patrick had watched soldiers in the field unload huge, heavy equipment with record speed when necessary and knew it was more than possible. As Chris described what happened when he arrived at the Army's base, Patrick already knew this part of the story but let him talk anyway.

Finally, Patrick and Evie thanked Chris and the three walked back toward his Jeep. Approaching where the lawnmower was being worked on, Patrick stopped, glancing down. "You need some help?"

"You know anything about small engines?" Chris asked, his voice laced with a mixture of doubt and hopefulness.

Chuckling as he squatted, Patrick nodded. "I figure my Gramps and I took apart, then put back together, quite a few in my younger days."

"Well, sure," Chris acknowledged. "I was cleaning a few parts, but am having a bit of trouble getting 'em back together."

For the next twenty minutes, Patrick and Chris worked side by side, re-assembling the old mower. With a couple of pulls on the starter cord, it roared to life. Chris shook Patrick's hand before moving it across the grass next to the driveway.

Evie had watched the men working while sitting in a nearby lawn chair in the shade, fascinated at the glimpse of Patrick in this environment. He was at ease...comfortable. A flashback, of her father mowing their small yards on the military bases, flew through her mind. Different years...different yards to mow. But always home. Her parents always made each place they lived feel like home.

Walking over, Patrick could tell Evie was lost in thought and, by the gentle smile on her face, he hoped she was thinking about him. Her gaze jumped to his as he approached and her smile widened. *Well, if she wasn't thinking about me, that's still a great reaction.*

Saying nothing on the drive home, they headed into her condo after picking up hamburgers at a drive-through. Evie grabbed plates and put the burgers and fries onto them, squirting the ketchup into a little pile by the fries. Patrick grinned down at the neat presentation of fast-food hamburgers.

Looking up, she cocked her head to the side. "What are you grinning at?"

Stepping forward, he kissed the top of her head, controlling his desire to pull her into his arms. "Just think you're cute, that's all. Never seen anyone spend so much time making burgers and fries from a drive-through look so fancy."

"Hmph," she groused, pretending to be offended while secretly loving the show of affection. It was so hard battling her growing feelings for him. *Oh, why does he have to be moving away?*

After the lunch was consumed, the two settled back on her sofa again and began to dissect Chris' accounting of the delivery.

"You don't believe him?" Evie asked in surprise.

"Didn't say that, but just because he reported that he was given the wrong address doesn't mean he was."

"Oh," she said, confusion marring her expression. "Then how do you know what's real and when someone is lying if nobody wants to tell the truth?"

Laughing, he said, "This is part of the puzzle solving. I think this is why I'd like the investigating side of things."

"But puzzle solving with materials is easier," she complained. "Measurements, equations, the mathematics, the physics of a problem will eventually present the solutions. People?" she huffed. "They don't fit the same structural dimensions."

"No, they don't," he agreed, still smiling as he watched her adorable face trying to puzzle out the solution.

"So what's next?" she asked. "How do we find out whether or not Chris was telling the truth?"

Sobering, Patrick thought for a moment. "Well, I can ask the Saints for any assistance in getting into files and records of the shipment. Monty told me that Luke, their computer guru, can get all the info needed from a computer, but it requires someone to insert a specialized thumb drive first."

"I could do that," Evie enthused, sitting up straighter.

"Oh, hell no," Patrick growled. "No fuckin' way!"

Slumping back down, she said, "Then what'll we do?"

Pulling out his phone, he sent a text to Monty and within a few minutes received a call. He went over the interview with Chris and then listened as Monty gave him new instructions. Disconnecting, he turned back to Evie, a wide grin on his boyish face.

"Seems the Saints can find out all sorts of things. Can I borrow your laptop, babe?"

Evie nodded and walked over to her small desk and picked it up. *Babe.* She had to admit the endearment made her smile. Turning back to him, she handed him the laptop. "What are you going to do?"

"Gonna send Monty the names of some people at GMS and Luke can start checking their computers. He can't get as much info as if we had direct access, but it'll give us something."

Evie rattled off the few names she knew from the plant, including Ed's. Patrick looked up, asking about the people she worked with.

Her eyes widened with the implication that someone in the military sales department would be involved in theft. Her face fell, as she considered the thought. Her shoulders drooping, she said, "This really could have been an inside job, couldn't it?"

Patrick set the laptop on the coffee table, moving closer to her. He wrapped his arms around her body, pulling her into his warmth. She mumbled into his chest, but the words were indiscernible. Pushing her back ever so slightly, he peered questioningly into her eyes.

"I hate the thought that it could be someone I know," she repeated, as he nodded, silently agreeing.

She became aware of his arms around her, the feel of his strength seeping in. Her soft curves crushed against the hard planes of his body. *This feels right. This feels good. This feels...the way it should.* Heaving a sigh, she pushed herself away and settled back against the sofa cushions, forcing herself to remember that he was leaving. Her hand moved toward her chest, rubbing gently. *Why does this hurt now?* Blinking, trying to overcome the sting of tears, she fought to maintain her composure, but the answer was staring her in the face. *It hurts because we're already friends. And could be more...if only.*

"You okay, babe?"

Nodding quickly, she offered a wobbly smile. "Yeah, just overwhelmed, that's all."

"Investigating someone close to you isn't easy," he conceded.

She knew he thought she was referring to the investigation...when it was her heart she was battling. "Yeah..." Sitting up straighter, she said, "Okay, Captain Courageous, what do I need to do?"

Laughing, they settled in to finish the list for Luke and continued planning. The afternoon weaved its way into the evening and she fixed a quick dinner, insisting he stay. The conversation was lively...the silences were easy.

As he walked to the door, when the evening was over, he turned and gazed at her standing in the living room. Their eyes locked. Longing...and hoping...passed between them. Slowly he opened his arms wide, the invitation stated.

She hesitated for a moment, warring between staying professional and safe...or possibly opening herself to heartbreak. It only took a moment, then her body acted on its own...tired of waiting on her mind. She rushed over, throwing herself into his arms, feeling them wrap around her, pulling her tight. Holding on... saying nothing.

He kissed the top of her head, murmuring, "Tried to stay away, babe. But what we have is special...it's something we could build on."

"How, when you're leaving?" she whispered, her eyes tearing once more as she peered up into his. She felt her body move as he heaved a huge sigh.

"Don't know. I fuckin' don't know. I just know that I want you in my life," he vowed honestly.

She nodded against his chest as he kissed her hair once more. Offering him a watery smile, she watched as he walked out her door. Closing it softly, she allowed the tears to slide down her cheeks.

10

Rolling over in bed, Evie looked at the clock. Another sleepless night had her restless...and needing advice. She knew her mother rose early each morning. A habit born out of necessity from years of being an Army wife, where she made sure to awake with her husband to prepare him a hearty breakfast before he left in the pre-dawn hours to go to work when he was stationed stateside.

"Hey, Mom," Evie greeted, having made the decision to call.

"Sweetie! How are you?"

Evie reveled in the familiar sound...the warmth...the joy of hearing her mother's voice. Suddenly, missing her, she choked, "I need to talk, mom."

"Oh, honey, what's going on?"

Sucking in a deep breath, Evie sat up in bed and pushed the pillows behind her. Sniffing, she asked, "Mom, how hard was it...with dad? You know...moving all the time...never knowing where you'd end up."

Silence greeted her for a moment before her mother replied, "It was good sometimes…" and with a small chuckle, she added, "and really bad sometimes. Just like you and your sister, I had to make new friends, keep changing my job, trying to make each place a home. But then I had the chance to visit some amazing places… meet people that I would have never met if I'd stayed in my little hometown." She was silent for a second and then asked, "What's got you thinking about that so early this morning?"

"I don't know…" she lied, trying to figure out what she wanted to say.

"I think you do," her mother interjected, "and I have a feeling it must be because you met someone."

Snorting, Evie said, "Yeah…I should have known you'd see through this."

"Well, tell me all about it," her mother prompted.

Evie began, hesitantly at first, then with more depth, about meeting Patrick, going from not liking him, to their budding friendship, to their investigation, and finishing up with him moving to Virginia.

"I agree, honey. That's tough and you know I can't tell you what to do, especially when you're about to land the job you've been waiting for. But, I will just say that I knew being a military brat was harder on you than the rest of us. I understand how much you longed to put down roots and stay in one place, so I'm not about to tell you to move to the other side of the country for this man. Unless you love him…and then, only you can decide if it's worth picking up your life and moving."

"Mom, I've got a good job here. I...well, I don't have a lot of friends...but I like my job...well, I should like it when I move into the engineering position next month. And I like my place...well, I'm only subletting, but I know I'll like making my own home when I get it." Hearing herself say the words out loud, she hung her head. "Oh, mom, I don't sound very sure, do I?"

Her mother's smile could be felt through the phone, as she said, "It's okay, Evie. You're young. You don't need to have your whole life planned right now. You always wanted everything outlined so that you wouldn't be surprised by anything. That was the budding engineer in you. But life is full of surprises...new adventures...new trails to blaze...new people to meet. You always saw change as a bad thing, something to fear. But sometimes, change opens us up to adventures we never knew we could experience."

"Did you ever regret choosing dad?" she asked tentatively.

"Oh, no, sweetie. Yes, there were challenges and there was heartache. And losing your dad on his last tour was the biggest heartache of all. But I accepted him for who he was—he was a soldier. So I accepted all that went with it."

A thoughtful silence settled between mother and daughter, each to their own thoughts for a moment, before her mom continued, "I'm not telling you to give up your life in California for this man. I'm only telling you that you have to make the choice. If staying in California is what you want to do, then by all means do that.

But if you have feelings for this man, and staying in California is only a safe choice...then maybe you need to step out of your comfort zone. Safe can be good...but it can also keep you from the adventures that are waiting out there for you. I never regretted the adventures with your dad, sweetie."

"I love you, mom," Evie said, new tears sliding down her cheeks.

"And I love you, baby girl," came the familiar reply.

Disconnecting, Evie looked at the rising sun and wished for answers to the swirling questions in her mind to simply appear.

A text sounded and she smiled as she looked down, seeing Patrick's name. **Morning beautiful. Spent all night thinking of you.**

Me too, she texted back.

Can I see you tonite?

Grinning, she could not deny her heart leaped at the thought. **Absolutely!**

Pick u up at 6. Be safe today.

Leaning back on the pillows, the sun was now peeking over the tops of the trees, illuminating her bedroom in a soft pink glow. Smiling, she thought, *Maybe, just maybe...*

Determined to discover if she could find out more, Evie began to check on the past year's requisitions made to the Army Corps of Engineers, then expanded her search to others. While transoms and side panels were large items, there were other shipments of much smaller items packed in boxes. Easy for someone to miss in a shipment. What she found astounded her. There had been five large claims of missing items from a variety of clients over the past eighteen months. *And no one is following up on this? What the hell is going on?*

With righteous indignation, she stormed out of her office and down the hall to Saul. Entering without knocking, she plopped down in his chair, tossing the files on his desk.

He looked up in surprise, saying, "Well, hello to you too! Whatcha got there?"

"I want someone to explain why this company is dealing with theft and no one is asking the tough questions."

He scanned the reports and looked up, a curious expression on his face. "Evelyn, I've got to ask, why are you checking into these? This was before you were hired."

"I just want to do what's right, Saul. Is there a theft problem?"

Sighing, he said, "Look, I realize you're an engineer and not trained in sales, but you need to understand that every company has a certain amount of loss due to theft, misdirected shipments, breakage, damage, order error...lots of reasons."

"And is there not a way to check into these things?" she pushed.

"Of course," he replied. "I know for damage and

breakage, depending on where it occurred, Ed is in charge of getting the reports to quality control. For shipments, he deals with the paperwork for that as well. Thefts...well, if it can be determined that there is a culprit, then we would let them go."

Shock flashed across her face as she asked, "Just let them go? What about the fact that they committed a crime"?"

Saul blushed and rushed to say, "Well, we'd also turn them over to the police, of course." Sighing heavily, he ran his hand over his face before looking directly at her again. "Honestly, Evelyn, I've never had to deal with something like this before."

Evie was silent for a moment as her mind continued to process the problem. "Has anyone even checked with the warehouse that the sub driver ended up going to mistakenly?"

Saul looked up, eyes narrowed, "How do you know about that?"

The two sat silently, staring at each other before jumping when Gary entered the room. He sat down in the chair next to Evie and glared at both of them for a moment. She cocked her head to the side in question before glancing between the two brothers, sensing a silent communication. Running her tongue over her suddenly dry lips, she waited to see what Gary wanted.

"Evelyn," Gary began. "I appreciate you wanting to understand what's going on around here, but I've had three people coming to me reporting that you have been asking questions about past shipments."

"I'm just inquiring—"

He held up his hand, "I get that. I know you're not making any accusations, but you've got to stop. Just do your sales job until the career change to the engineering job next month...or..."

Her eyes jumped to his sharply, aware that Saul's gaze moved to his brother's as well. "Or what?" she asked, holding her breath, afraid of the response.

Gary, jerking on his necktie to loosen it a bit, his face contorted as he sighed. "Look, Evelyn, you have to be a team player here, if you want to continue."

Eyes now widening in shock, she clarified, "Are...are you saying what I think you're saying? If I keep trying to track down what happened to that missing shipment... an error that cost this company a lot of money...then I won't get the engineering job? Or might lose my job completely?" Her voice rose with each word, her naturally soft-spoken manner overcome with incredulity.

"Gary," Saul warned, shaking his head slowly.

"Look, it's not just me. It's dad. The idea of negative publicity has him really on edge." Turning to look at Evie, he continued, "This isn't a threat, but you've got to consider the whole picture. It's our decision to investigate or not...not yours. If we, as the company, decide to take the loss, then you need to accept it and move on."

"The military needs our equipment," she argued back. "They need it when they need it, not when we refill an order because it got stolen...or lost...or misplaced."

"And I'm telling you that it's not your concern," he bit out.

"I care about this company," she stated emphatically.

"I care about its reputation. And as an Army brat, I also care about the military getting their equipment." For the first time, Evie realized she was proud of being a soldier's daughter. *So what if we moved around...my dad was a hero and our family stood for that.*

Standing from his chair, appearing uncomfortable, and said, "I don't have a problem with your dedication to being a military brat, but if you care about this company's reputation...and yours...then you'll settle down and do your job." With that, he walked out leaving her seething.

The silence between Evie and Saul was now deafening, neither speaking for several long minutes. He looked at her, his expression grim.

"I'm sorry, Evelyn," he said, frustration lacing his voice. "I don't know what to say that'll make you feel any better."

Sitting perfectly still to quell the desire to cry, Evie said nothing.

"I know this is difficult, but I can tell you that from years in the Financial Department, it is common for companies to take losses, whether in production, sales, deliveries...whatever. If it were of epic proportions, then the company would have to take the time to investigate, but for the occasional loss...we just write it off."

"Saul, that answer is not good enough for me."

His face contorted as he begged, "Please, let it go. I don't want to lose your friendship...or working with you."

Standing, she offered him a small shrug. "I don't know what to say. I've got some hard thinking to do."

With that, she turned and walked down the hall to her office. Once there, she sat at her desk, the past half-hour rolling through her thoughts. *They'd really fire me for trying to solve a theft? All the talk about wanting my engineering skills would just be tossed away?*

Heaving a sigh, she looked at the clock on her computer. *Only eleven a.m. Great...I still have five more hours to just get through this day!*

Patrick fidgeted as he waited to be patched in for a video-conference with the Saints. Suddenly, Monty came onto the screen, a wide grin on his face.

"Good to see you, man," Monty greeted.

"You too," Patrick agreed, glad for the meeting to start. The camera panned around, introducing the other Saints, before landing on Jack Bryant.

"Captain Cartwright," Jack acknowledged with a nod.

"Call me Patrick. The Captain will be retired in a couple of months."

"And do I hope you'll join us then?" Jack inquired.

Grinning, Patrick nodded. "I'd like to. I thought once I can get this matter taken care of, I'll visit my sister and parents and talk to you about the Saints."

With his usual curt nod, Jack agreed then turned the meeting over to Luke, whose fingers had been flying on his keyboard.

"I've gone through the emails of the major players that were on Evie's list. Gary, Saul, and Ed in particular.

I've widened my scope to include the others as well. And just to let you know, I've been in contact with Dane Logan, your friend Chris's computer expert. He's agreed to assist, saying any friend of Chris's is a friend of his. So you've got a lot of backup on this. Now, the bad news is that so far, I do not see anything unusual in their work or personal emails, nor their bank accounts."

"Damn!" Patrick cursed. "I was hoping something would show up on someone from her company."

"Hold on," Luke admonished. "We're still working the problem."

"You'll find that patience will be your best friend in this business…and sometimes your worst enemy," Jack advised. "We chase down a lot of leads before finding the right one."

Patrick nodded, grimacing. *Fuck, I'm not doing very well for my first investigation and meeting with the Saints.* Sitting up straighter in his chair, he peered at the laptop screen, determined to pay close attention to what Luke was saying.

"Now, I did start running a preliminary check on the warehouse you said the truck driver stopped at. It seems to be somewhat buried in layers of ownership, which is not necessarily unusual, but can also indicate someone trying to hide who really owns or runs the place."

"Would it help if I could get in there?" Patrick asked. He noticed the grins right away from Monty and Jack. The camera swung around to a large Hispanic man, sitting next to Monty.

"Patrick, I'd like to introduce you to Cam. He's our

best at...uh...entering facilities, and I don't mean through the front door."

Cam nodded his greeting and said, "Jack's arranged a little trip for me. I know Monty and Angel were going to fly out to see you, so we've moved their trip up and I'll come as well if that works for you. Marc's a pilot and he'll bring us, so you don't need to meet us anywhere."

The thrill of the hunt coursed through Patrick as he realized how dedicated the Saints were. "Jack, I don't know how to thank you—"

"You don't need to thank us," Jack interrupted. "You know I was Army Special Forces, just like you, and some of my men are former military. We know what it was like to be in a warzone without all our equipment. Nothin' pisses us off more than our brothers who can't be protected 'cause some asshole stole it to sell on the black market. We'd do this for you even if you weren't considering joining us."

Nodding, chest swelling with pride, Patrick agreed. Settling upon the details of the mission, they disconnected. Leaning back in his seat, he swiveled around to peer out of his window once more. Seeing the soldiers moving equipment, he smiled. *Now, we're going to make a fuckin' difference.* His mind moved to Evie, and his grin grew wider.

Placing a call to Chris, he brought him up to speed on what was happening and thanked him for contacting his computer expert, Dane. "It appears that Dane and Luke work well together."

"Appreciate it, man," Patrick said. "The more people

working on this, the better chance we have of finding out about the missing shipment."

"No problem," Chris replied. "Missing military equipment...especially stolen military equipment, meant for the war zones, pisses us right-the-fuck-off!"

With vows to get together soon, they disconnected, leaving Patrick feeling more and more like a new career in investigation might be just what he needed.

———

Evie snapped her laptop shut at the exact moment her workday was over. Snatching her purse from the drawer, she threw it over her shoulder and stalked down the hall. The hours since her meeting that morning had done nothing to quell her anger. She had moved through the emotions of fury, indecision, hurt, betrayal, and finally ended right back at anger again.

She heard her name called and, recognizing Saul's voice, kept on walking. Stopping only when she arrived at her car, she jumped in and pealed out of the parking lot. Behind her, in the building, Saul and Gary peered down at her.

"Did you have to threaten her job?" Saul growled, his own anger undisguised.

"Look, you know how dad hates negative publicity," Gary retorted. "The last thing we need is for her to be digging into things that don't concern her." Noting his brother's silence, he turned, saying, "What's with you? I thought she made it clear she didn't date co-workers."

"I know, but that doesn't keep me from really liking

her. Not to mention, we've wanted her on board as an engineer anyway. Now, who knows what she'll do."

The two men sighed as they turned from the window. Staring at the street she drove down would not solve their problems.

11

"Hey, Evie," Patrick greeted, answering his phone.

"I want you to come to my place," Evie jumped in. "I need to see you."

Now alert, he asked, "What's wrong? What's happened?"

"Just come straight to my place after work. Can you do that for me?" she begged.

"Of course. I'll be there in about fifteen minutes." Hearing her disconnect, he gunned his engine a little faster, matching his heartbeat. *Something's up...what the fuck happened today?*

Patrick jogged up the stairs to Evie's condo door, anxious to see her. He lifted his hand to knock when the door was flung open and her hands darted out, grabbing his shirt.

Jerking him in, she launched herself at him as she slammed the door and with as much force as she could muster, plastered her body to his front. With both hands on his square jaw, she pulled him down for a kiss, not waiting for him to speak.

Stunned, Patrick welcomed her luscious body pressed up to his, wrapping his arms around her. She surprised him again when she jumped up and he caught her with one hand under her ass for support.

"Babe...Evi—"

She refused to allow him to speak, wanting her lips and her body to do the talking. Owning the kiss, she slipped her tongue into his mouth, the taste intoxicating. Sucking on his tongue, she heard him moan...*or maybe that came from me.*

Whirling around, Patrick pressed her back against the front door, their bodies pressed tightly from hip to head. He allowed her to take charge of the kiss for a moment, reveling in the delicious sensation of her tongue tangling with his, her breasts crushed against his chest, and her pelvis grinding against his erection.

Moving her hands from his face, she fumbled with the buttons on his shirt—at least the ones she could reach. Sliding her hands down, she jerked his shirttails out of his pants. His buckle was proving to be more difficult so her hands found their way back to his shoulders where she tried to push the offending material away.

Reality taking root, Patrick moved back slightly, his lust filled eyes attempting to focus on the woman in his arms. Mewling at the loss of contact, she ground her hips into his.

"Evie babe, slow down, slow down," he said, gulping air as desire coursed through his body.

"I don't want to slow down. I don't want to stop," she moaned trying to press tighter against him. "Don't you want this?"

"You know I do," he rasped. Twisting away from the door, he moved to the sofa with her still in his arms. "But I want it to be real, not a reaction to whatever is goin' on inside your head."

Tucking her face in his neck, she breathed him in, his rejection stinging. "I'm sorry—"

"No, no. Don't be sorry. Girl, you've got to know I want this with you. I've wanted this with you for a while now."

"So what's holding you back?" she whispered, her face still buried.

"Talk to me first, Evie. Something's happened and I want to know what. I know you have feelings for me, but until now, the fact that I'm leaving has put a stop to you wanting to see what we could become." He gently pulled her face from his neck and, pushing her long hair back from her forehead, held her gaze. "Don't get me wrong, baby. I'm loving every second of having your mouth on mine, your body pressed against mine, and swear to God, I thought I was going to come in my pants the way we were grinding. But I gotta know what's changed."

She dropped her eyes, staring at his chin, not willing to see his doubts. Heaving a huge sigh, she shifted her body to move off of his.

"Uh uh," he said, smiling. "I like you right here." Then, seeing the tortured expression on her face, he softened his voice as he pulled her in for a hug. "Come on, Evie. Tell me what's going on."

"It's...complicated," she confessed.

"Got all night, baby."

"I don't even know where to start," she replied, her fingers absentmindedly fidgeting with his shirt collar.

"How about the beginning?"

Her gaze jumped to his, seeing nothing but concern. Licking her lips slowly, she nodded. "I promised myself when I got out of college, I wasn't going to be like my dad—always moving. I wanted stability. You know, the kind that comes with staying in one place. Getting to know my neighbors. Finding a favorite pizza place. Having a yard that I could plant flowers in and then see them the next year when they bloomed." She hesitated for a moment, weighing her words. "Then I met you."

"But you didn't like me at first," he reminded, the corners of his eyes crinkling at the memory.

Smiling, she said, "Well, after the first meeting. You're gorgeous, sexy, fun, smart—"

"Whoa, then how'd you stay away from my awesomeness?" he teased, brushing her dark hair back away from her face again, this time leaving his hand cupping the back of her head. Her hair felt like silk and he fisted his fingers through the strands.

Now chuckling, she pretended to swat his shoulder. "It wasn't easy." Sobering, she sought his gaze and continued, "The fact that you were in the Army was actually a strike against you. Then you said you were getting out and I thought we might have a chance. Then you said you were moving and I knew then that we'd have nothing to build upon."

"And now?"

"The more time I spend with you, the more I really like you." She sighed heavily again. "I felt conflicted... like I was in a battle with myself. The plans I had made with what was now in front of me that I wanted."

Her fingers continued to play with his shirt, almost driving him to distraction, but he wanted her to feel comfortable enough to touch him...talk to him... confide in him.

"I called my mom this morning," she confessed. She saw his lifted eyebrow and hastened to explain. "I told her about you. And I asked about my dad. About how it was for her to move and not put down roots."

"What did she say?" he asked, curiosity overcoming his nervousness.

Boldly keeping her eyes on his, she said, "Mom loved dad. So she accepted everything about him. His deployments. The moves. Everything. She said she wouldn't have had it any other way except to have him come home after his last tour."

Patrick knew Evie was struggling with something profound and her actions spoke of this battle. Staring at the woman in his arms, he hoped she trusted him enough to reveal what was in her heart. *Come on, baby. I need more. I need you to be sure.*

"Mom told me that I always wanted to have my life planned out so I wouldn't have any surprises, but she said it was all right to have adventures. Especially if you're with someone you love."

At the word *love*, he sucked in a breath and then saw the doubt pass through her eyes. "Keep talking, babe. Say whatever you need to say and I promise, I'm right here."

Blushing, she admitted, "Well, I'm not saying that I love you…but…I really like you…a lot."

Gliding his hands through her hair, he moved them to cup the sides of her head. "I'm glad, Evie. So fuckin' glad to hear you say that." He paused for a moment before prodding, "But I know there's more. What happened today?"

Pushing off his lap, she began to pace the floor, her body needing to work off the emotions burning through her. "I've had almost seven hours to think about everything. I was so angry at first. How dare they? I was furious, livid, pissed off and wanted to kick some GMS butt!"

His lips curved ever so slightly at the emphatic threats his girl was making. *His girl? Hell yeah! Whether or not she knew it…she was his girl.*

"Then I was upset, thought about quitting, thought about playing nice and doing what they said, and then I was right back to being angry again." She stopped pacing and turned sharply, facing him once more. "And then I thought about what my mom said this morning."

Cocking his head to the side, he said nothing, simply allowing her the opportunity to come to her own conclusion.

"I've been battling the feelings I have for you. The ones you want to build on, but I wanted to stay safe more than take a chance. I thought if I stayed in one place, then I'd be safe. I'd be happy. I thought I'd be in control." Shrugging while throwing her hands up to the side, she added, "But today showed me that no matter how much I plan...life changes all around me. So, I either let it just happen to me or I decide to come out of my safe zone myself and take some chances."

Standing, Patrick stalked over to Evie, stopping when his polished, military shoes met her tiny toes. Towering over her, he reached up to cup her soft face, seeing her eyes search his. "Baby, I promise, I'll always be a safe place for you. You decide to take a chance...I'll be your safe harbor and your adventure. You decide to build on this friendship and I'll tell you, I'm already with you. You decide to fall, Evie girl...I'll always catch you."

Leaning into his hand, she closed her eyes as the warmth of his palm caressed her face. She felt his other hand come to rest on her waist, gently pulling in so that her body leaned against him. And she made the choice to fall.

Patrick lifted Evie back into his arms, feeling her legs wrap around his waist. Remembering the way she had greeted him at the door already had his dick hard and ready. Her warm center, now once more pressing against his erection, only made it sweeter this time. Walking toward her bedroom, he let her body slide down his slowly once reaching the bed. Pressed tightly against him, their gazes held for a moment, then her eyes lowered to his shirt, still mostly unbuttoned, and her fingers moved to complete the task.

Pushing the material off his shoulders, she let the shirt hit the floor. Her eyes followed its path and she looked up, concern in her eyes. "Should I...um...hang it up?"

Chuckling, he shook his head, cupping both of her cheeks in his hands. "I think it's fine if it gets wrinkled. There's no regulation that says my shirt can't lie on the floor...especially when it's gonna be joined by your clothes in about two seconds."

Her eyes dilated with lust as she lowered her gaze to his muscular chest, prominently displayed in the tight t-shirt. Her fingers traced his abdomen through the material before pulling it from his pants as well. Bunching it up in her hands, she raised it up to his chin before he reached back and snagged it over his head, tossing it onto the floor.

Oh my, God, she thought, seeing his naked chest up close. *Seeing it from a distance at the pool had been eye-catching, but this?* Her breath whooshed out as her fingers trailed along the ridges of his chest and abdomen. She recognized his dog tags, but it was the silver medallion hanging around his neck that had her curious. Lifting it in her fingers, she read the inscription. St. Patrick.

"My Gramps gave that to me when I graduated from college."

"It's lovely," she admitted, turning the pendant over in her hand.

"St. Patrick is the Patron Saint of Engineers."

At that, her gaze jumped from the emblem to his eyes. "That would make him my Patron Saint as well," she smiled.

"Gramps taught me that it takes time, patience, and care to build something, and then to protect what I built. He said that I'd be good at that." Patrick hesitated for a moment, saw her smile and continued, "He also said the same thing would work for people as well as machines."

"Is that what we're doing now?" she whispered.

His answer was sealing his lips over hers. Plunging his tongue into her sweetness, he stoked the flames roaring back to life.

Her fingers moved down to his belt, making quick work of it until his hand stilled her motion. He reached down, pulling her t-shirt up, forcing her hands to lift into the air as the garment slid off her body. Hooking his thumbs into the waistband of her yoga pants, he slid them down, snagging her panties along the way, as she unhooked her bra and added it to the ever-growing pile of clothes on the floor.

Standing completely naked, she was self-conscious for only a second before seeing the unmasked look of approval and lust on his face. Grinning, she backed up to the bed and sat on the edge. Lifting her feet to the mattress, she scooted herself backward until she was in the center.

Lust now rushing through his body, Patrick toed off his shoes and then jerked off his pants and boxers. Leaning forward as he placed his hands on the mattress, his cock stood at attention, already leaning toward her with a mind of its own. *Gotta wait, boy. Gotta take this slow and make it perfect for her.*

Crawling over her body, he laid down beside her, his gaze roaming over her perfection from her smooth skin, over her full breasts, down to the treasure at the apex of her thighs. He trailed his hand over her body, feeling the silky smooth skin beneath his calloused fingertips. Her body responded to his touch and he grinned as her hips lifted naturally toward his hand as it slid between her legs.

Leaning over, he left a trail of kisses from her lips to the pulse at the base of her neck, and then down to her luscious breasts. Latching on to one nipple, he licked, tongued, sucked, and nipped at the swollen, sensitive bud.

Evie's hands grabbed the back of his head and she wished his hair, cut in the traditional short military haircut, was longer so she could grasp it in her fingers. Instead, she wrapped her hand around the back of his neck, encouraging him to continue his delicious torture.

Still sucking, he moved one hand down over her slightly rounded belly, to her slick folds. Slowly inserting one digit into her tight channel, he fingered her gently. Crooking deep inside, he knew he had hit the spot he wanted to find as her moans increased. Pulling a taut nipple into his mouth, he sucked hard, giving it a nip before soothing with his tongue.

Evie wanted to throw her head back but forced herself to continue to watch the man hovering over her, making her body sing. She felt every nerve. Every tingle. Every caress and suckle. And thought she would scream with need. Her body taut, she almost lifted from the bed as his thumb circled her clit. The pressure built until with one last tweak of his finger, she burst with electricity pulsating in all directions. He sucked her nipple as her head fell back against the pillow, a moan filling the spinning room.

He felt her inner walls clench, watched her gasp as her body shook with her orgasm and realized he had never seen anything as beautiful as a woman he cared about being pleasured.

Barely able to lift her head, she smiled as he placed his fingers into his mouth, wet with her juices, and sucked them. He moved back up over her body, his lips capturing hers once more. Tasting her essence on his tongue, she felt her womb clench once again and her hips rose in silent invitation.

Smiling, he brushed her damp hair away from her face, leaving a trail of wet kisses from her forehead down along her jaw, her lips captured. Owning the kiss, he plundered, sucked, tasted, taking her breath.

"I need you...now!" she managed to gasp, opening her legs wider.

"Anything for you, baby," he promised. Rolling to the side, he grabbed a condom that he had tossed to the pillow just before getting onto the bed. Rolling it on, he slid back over her body. With her legs spread for him, he stared down at her glistening sex and seated himself at her entrance.

He wanted to go slow, to savor every feeling, but one look at her lust-filled eyes, and the feel of her soft body underneath his, he lost all resolve. Plunging his erection to the hilt, he stopped as her sudden gasp met his ears. "Oh, baby, I'm sorry," he panted, starting to pull out.

"No, no, keep going," she begged. Evie was no virgin, although her experience was rather limited and it had been a while. *And no one was ever this size!* The feel of his girth against her tight walls created the perfect friction. *God, Yes!* her mind screamed, as her hands and legs clasped him tightly to her body, holding as though he would disappear.

He thrust slowly, allowing the moisture to slick her inner walls, easing the passage. As her core began to accept his aching cock, he pumped faster. Feeling her relax slightly underneath him he kissed her, his tongue moving in unison with his dick. Her moans filled his mouth as he moved faster and faster with ease.

Feeling his balls tighten, he slipped his hand down between them, resting his weight on his other bent arm.

All thoughts flew from her mind as the feeling of this man on top of her, joined with her as one, consumed her. The feeling of friction deep inside had every nerve tingling again, and she desperately wanted the sweet bliss she knew was coming. Tighter and tighter she coiled.

Moving his mouth down to suck on her nipple while his fingers clamped down on her swollen clit was all it took to take her over the edge. With her fingernails digging into his back he watched as she screamed out his name, her tight inner walls clamping down on his dick. He had never liked a woman's fingernail marks on his back before, not wanting any woman to have a claim once they parted, but this? *Fuckin' yeah.* He wanted to wear her marks for all to see, as he looked down at the love bite he had given her earlier. *Both marked. For each other.*

With only a few more thrusts he threw his head back, a grimace on his face as his neck corded with the force of his orgasm. Deeper and deeper. Finally, with every drop wrung out, he collapsed to the side, twisting with her in his arms, keeping her tightly in his embrace.

The lust momentarily spent, Patrick's mind rolled her earlier words over and over. *She'd been talking about something at work. Thinking about quitting. Damn, I was so overcome when she came on to me, we never finished talking about what happened.*

Her body limp next to his, he glanced down at her face. She looked...*well satisfied*, he thought, puffing his masculine pride. Her eyes were closed, thick lashes resting on her cheeks. Her well-kissed lips, plump and moist, and opened ever so slightly as her breathing evened. Hating to ruin the moment, he knew something had occurred besides the heart-to-heart phone conversation with her mother. "Evie?"

"Mmmmm," she replied, her body sated and boneless.

He lifted her chin with his fingers so her eyes met his. "You mentioned something about today and wanting to quit. Did something happen at work?"

She gazed over his shoulder for a moment before sliding her eyes back to his. "I was threatened at work toda—"

"What the fuck?" he shouted, jerking hard while pulling her body in closer.

"No, no, not like that," she hastened to say. "I mean my job was threatened."

His fury abated only by a smidgen and he growled, "Evie, I need you to tell me everything."

Huffing, she said, "You're not making this easy. I was talking earlier about feelings and you're getting all alpha macho." Seeing the unchanging expression on his face, she plunged ahead and explained the morning's meeting with Gary and Saul. "So essentially, my trying to do something good has now made them re-evaluate whether or not they want me there as an engineer."

Patrick's anger had not diminished during her explanation. GMS' management had him seeing red, but he knew she was continuing to struggle with her emotions so he kept his fury under control. *At least until I get a chance to find these assholes!*

12

Two days later, Evie waited nervously for her guests to arrive. Patrick had sent her address to Monty and the group arriving from Virginia were expected at any moment. Patrick came into the living room, saw her rearranging the magazines on the end table and walked over, placing his large hand on hers.

"Baby, it's gonna be—"

She jumped as the doorbell rang. Casting an uneasy glance his way, she offered a tremulous smile.

Squeezing her hands, they walked to the door together. The room filled with the three large men who entered, along with Patrick's beautiful sister. It did not take long for Evie to wonder why she had ever been concerned.

Angel rushed to sweep Evie into a huge hug, warm and sincere. "I'm so glad to meet someone who's so perfect for my brother. He's told us so much about you!"

Evie's eyes widened as she peered over Angel's shoulder to Patrick and was met with his wide grin.

Pulling back, she took in the fun appearance of his sister. Her long blonde hair was streaked with pink, purple, and teal stripes. She looked like a cupcake—exactly as he had described.

Angel's fiancé, Monty, introduced himself with a smile before throwing his arm around Angel. Marc, introduced as the pilot, was even larger than Patrick, and with his rugged handsomeness and thick beard, looked like he would be more at home in a cabin in the mountains. Then came Cam, an even larger Hispanic man, with an easy smile.

As the group moved into the living room, the doorbell sounded again. Opening the door, Evie was greeted by Chris and his wife Cherylenne, a soft-spoken, brunette beauty. She and Patrick had met them for dinner the evening before and Patrick invited them over for the planning. Hugging them both, she watched as Chris immediately integrated with the other men as if he had known them for years. She turned toward the women, introducing Cherylenne to Angel.

The five men sat down and began planning their evening activities. Evie wanted to hear what they were saying but felt her hostess duties included getting lunch ready for everyone.

Angel grinned and patted her shoulder. "I'll grab the drinks while you listen. Just tell me what to set out and you can stay."

Cherylenne agreed, saying, "Angel and I'll take care of everything. You go on in."

Shooting them a grateful look, she responded, "The chicken salad and roast beef slices are in the refrigerator. I was going to set them out with the potato salad, chips, and slaw."

"Got it, sweetie," Angel grinned and headed into the kitchen, arm in arm with Cherylenne.

Evie listened carefully to what the men were saying, but it soon became evident that she had no clue what they planned. Military terms were being bandied about, but she discerned that Patrick and the others would be breaking into the warehouse that evening and gathering information from the computers, in the hope that it would lead them back to the culprit at GMS.

Her stomach clenched at the thought and a gasp escaped before she could control her breathing. The men's gazes all jumped to her in concern.

"Babe—" Patrick said, starting to stand.

"No, no," she said quickly, holding her hand up. Looking at the men, she blushed. "I'm sorry. It just really hit me that this is happening." Seeing their questioning expressions, she hastened to explain. "I've been in the middle of this mess for weeks now and just recently…" her eyes cut to Patrick's, "had my job threatened if I don't stop trying to find out what happened—"

"What the fuck?" Cam growled, leaning forward in his seat, his eyes piercing hers.

Chris cast his gaze between Evie and Patrick, a glower on his face matching the other men's.

Giving a little shrug, she looked back over at Patrick, seeing his warm expression on her. "Let's just say that it gave me a lot to think about."

Monty spoke up, "Patrick, Evie. We can stop this right now. We don't have to do anything. No problem, no worries. None of us want you to lose your job over this."

Smiling at his sincerity, she shook her head. "No, I want you here. I thought about it and I'm not afraid of losing my job. In fact, if that's the kind of place GMS is, then it makes me question whether I want to continue my employment there anyway." Looking at each person in the room, almost giving in to a nervous giggle at the sight of the four large men settled in her small living room, "All I meant was just that it hit me how real this is. But please, continue. I want to get to the bottom of this."

With a grin toward Patrick and catching his wink, she moved to the kitchen to help Angel and Cherylenne. "I should apologize," she said, "leaving you in my kitchen to fix lunch."

Laughing, Angel replied, "Oh, sweetie, I've been where you are! I was threatened a few months ago and believe me, Monty would have moved heaven and earth to get to the bottom of it. He and all the Saints."

"Same here," Cherylenne admitted, with a smile. "They're just like Chris and his SEAL brothers."

"Sounds like an interesting group of men," Evie said thoughtfully.

"None better," Angel enthused. "And Patrick will fit right in with the Saints. Dedicated, inquisitive, intelligent, and throw in a bit of an alpha when it comes to his woman!"

"Oh, I wouldn't say I'm his woman—"

"Evie, you don't know it yet, but you already are!"

Her eyes jumped to Angel's and Evie bit the corner

of her lip. "I confess, I didn't want to have anything to do with him when I found out he was in the military, and then again when he said he was moving to Virginia."

Angel's gaze softened and she turned from her task, setting down the bowl she had been carrying. "I'm sure that was hard. Afterall, your life is here. Have you thought about what you want to do? Try a long-distance relationship?"

Shaking her head, Evie said, "I don't think that would work, do you? I mean, we're talking about California and Virginia...opposite sides of the country." Glancing back into the living room, she watched as Patrick enthusiastically planned the mission with the others. "I could never hold him back from this," she admitted. Turning back to Angel, she said, "I guess I'll just have to figure out exactly what I'll do. But I know one thing," she grinned, "I'm crazy about your brother."

Smiling, the women finished the simple lunch and took it into the living room, listening as the men continued to plan.

That night, dressed all in black with a cap pulled over his blond hair, Patrick got his first up-close view of Cam's breaking and entering skills and was amazed. *Damn the man is good!* Missions in the Special Forces often involved the same skills, but from what he understood, Cam's were developed as a youth in a gang in El Paso, Texas. Grinning, he quietly followed the big man as they made their way down the back alleys of the dock warehouses. He watched as Cam easily by-passed the security system, with Luke's assistance from back in Virginia and Marc's technical skills as well.

Walking through the barely-lit halls, they quickly entered offices and hooked up their specialized thumb drives to the computers, allowing Luke to essentially be able to read anything that had been placed on the hard drives.

While Monty and Cam worked with the computers, Marc and Patrick did a search of the large warehouse. Moving amongst the tall wooden crates, they found nothing out of the ordinary. Patrick stood for a moment and whispered, "You know, if this warehouse company were part of the black market, they'd be using more than one distributor." With his hand resting on one of the crates, he said, "I wonder what's in these?"

Marc grinned and grabbed a crowbar propped against the wall, next to other tools. "Let's find out," he answered excitedly. With some leverage, he managed to pop the top off one of the crates, his muscles straining against the wood. Peering in together, they carefully moved the straw packing material to the side...exposing M4 Carbines. Whistling at the find, Marc and Patrick eyed each other.

Used heavily by the U.S. military, he knew that just because they were in this warehouse did not mean they were stolen—at least, not necessarily. Putting the lid back on, after snapping pictures of the weapons, Marc made quick work of nailing the lid down.

Cam and Monty met them in the corner and were

filled in on their find. Monty nodded, saying, "We need to get these drives back to Luke and I'll call Mitch to let him know what we've found."

Patrick looked questioningly at Monty, who explained that Mitch Evans was an FBI agent located in their area. "He'll know who to contact with the Sacramento branch of the FBI to get them involved."

With that agreement, the four men slipped unnoticed back into the dark alley. Patrick's thoughts swirled on the way to the hotel, where they left Evie and Angel. What appeared to be a random loss of a shipment, then seemed to be the work of someone at GMS, now had the probability of being a full-scale black market for military equipment.

Evie and Angel opened the door, taut nerves easy to read on their faces. Patrick stalked directly to Evie, wrapping her in his embrace while Monty moved instinctively to Angel. Marc and Cam pushed past the couples, grins on their faces.

Angel looked up and smiled, saying, "I can tell you all had a good evening!"

Evie watched in curiosity as the men, pumped from a successful mission, joked and laughed amongst themselves.

Cam walked over to Evie, bending to kiss her cheek. "Thanks for a good time," he chuckled. "We'll let Luke talk to Patrick here and the Saints'll find out what they can. Marc and I'll be flying out in the pre-dawn hours, so I'll say goodbye now. Hope to see you in Virginia."

Before she had a chance to respond, Marc came over, giving her a similar goodbye. "You've got a good man there. You two'll fit right in with the rest of us."

The two men headed out the door, leaving her and Patrick with Monty and Angel. Evie stood quietly with Patrick's arms around her as Monty turned to his fiancé. "Babe, we're still staying for a couple of days, but I've got to be on the phone for a while with Mitch."

"That's fine," Angel said. "I'm exhausted anyway."

Patrick and Evie walked to the door as well, the two women hugging. Monty shook Patrick's hand and grinned. "You did good tonight. Of course, you being Special Forces...I had no doubt. We'll come over tomorrow and I'll let you know what Mitch and Jack say." His eyes cut over to Evie and he smiled. "How about we take you guys out to eat tomorrow?"

"That'd be fine," she smiled, warmed by the couple's friendship and concern. With that, she and Patrick drove back over to her place.

Once there, Patrick followed her inside. He wanted to stay but was unsure how she felt. He watched as she eyed him from underneath her lashes and grinned. Her long, dark hair hung over her shoulders and as she slipped off her shoes, he realized once again how petite she was compared to him. Deciding to take matters into his own hands, he walked over and stilled her nervous fidgeting. "Babe, you've got to know that I want to stay."

Her gaze jumped to his in surprise, seeing his

smiling face peering down at her. "Oh, I really wanted you to, but didn't know if it was…uh…well, too clingy."

Throwing his head back, he responded, "No one could ever accuse you of being clingy, Evie. Not after I've had to work so hard to build us to where we are!"

Giggling, she pretended to slap at him but found her hand trapped in his as he wrapped his arms around her, lifting her off the ground. Easily hauling her into the bedroom, he gently tossed her onto the bed, following quickly. Holding his weight off her by leaning on his forearms, he owned her mouth. Raining kisses on her face, he then captured her giggling mouth once again, as the two began the slow, erotic dance of lovers.

"Close?"

"Yes…"

With his tongue licking her wet sex just before nipping on her clit, Evie stared at Patrick's head between her legs. She once more wished his hair was long enough to grab, having to fist the sheets instead.

Pressing her head back into the pillow as far as she could, Evie screamed out Patrick's name as her orgasm slammed into her, harder than she ever remembered. Quaking jolts shot from where his tongue worked its magic outward to every nerve in her body. Panting, she was barely aware as he maneuvered his Adonis body up over hers.

He grinned, seeing the sated expression on her face as it began to relax and a slow smile crept across her face. His cock strained toward her soft entrance, wanting its chance to feel her pliant warmth enshrouding it.

Patrick waited until her dark eyes opened and, for a second, halted as the depths of her feelings shone toward him. Capturing her lips, he sealed their fate with a kiss of the promise of a future.

Wrapping her limp arms around his waist, she tugged to gain his attention. "Don't make me wait another second. I need you inside me…now!"

"Hmmm, what shall I do with Miss Impatient?" he teased, his tongue still dancing around hers.

Giggling, she smiled as he fitted his cock against her entrance and her ready body welcomed him.

Gently at first, then thrusting harder and harder, all thoughts of teasing flew from his mind. Rocking into her, he tried to memorize her as their bodies became one, but the ever changing emotions crossing her face had him mesmerized. The combination of love and lust seemed to radiate from her, overwhelming at times. Closing his eyes, he powered through as his mind became melded with his cock and the goal of releasing inside of her warm, tight sex became overpowering.

With a few more thrusts, his balls tightened and he managed to open his eyes, meeting hers, as he roared through his orgasm as her legs snapped around his, pulling him tighter. As she milked the last drop from him, he fell on top, heedless of his weight for a few seconds until managing to roll slightly to the side, pulling her with him.

As the night air slowly cooled their bodies, he jerked

the covers over them. No more words were spoken... none were needed. And sleep claimed the lovers.

Two days later, as they were saying goodbye to Angel and Monty, Evie felt as though she were saying farewell to good friends. In spite of the intrigue surrounding her, she could not remember the last time she had laughed so freely—utterly letting go and enjoying herself.

Alone in her apartment for a few minutes, while Patrick said a private goodbye to his sister, she looked around at her space. *When was the last time I had people over to my apartment? When was the last time I went out with friends, other than meeting a few co-workers for drinks...when I don't drink?* Her thoughts swirled as she stood rooted to the floor, realizing that her mother was right. It wasn't the building that made a home...*it's who's with you that makes a home.*

Hands touched her shoulders and she yelped as she whirled around, seeing Patrick standing there, a surprised expression on his face.

"I'm sorr—" she began.

"I'm sorr—" he said at the same time.

They laughed as she walked straight into his arms, snuggling her face against his chest. His steady heart beat against her cheek. Warm. Secure. Home. *Yeah...he feels like home.*

"You were lost in thought when I came in, Evie babe. Did you have a good time with my sister?"

Leaning her head back, she smiled up at him. "Absolutely. I haven't had that good a time with friends... maybe since college...and maybe not even then!"

He watched as a cloud moved through her eyes, and dipped his head lower. "You wanna tell me what's going on in that head of yours?"

Sucking her lips in, she wondered how he already knew her so well. "I...well, I..." Giving herself a mental shake, she plunged forward and said, "You're leaving and now...I realize what I'll miss when you're gone." Heart pounding, she wondered what he would say to her statement. Would he ask her to try to have a long distance relationship? Would he want to try to keep building whatever they were building? Would he—

"Babe...what we've got...what we are together...you gotta know, I want to keep it." He watched carefully to see her reaction, pleased when the light returned to her eyes. "I know we're still new and being with me is a risk that I never thought you'd take...but I was going to ask you to consider moving with me to Virginia in a couple of months."

Her eyes widened and she felt her arms jerk, instinctively pulling him closer as his words rocked her world.

"You don't need to say anything now...just think about it."

They stood, quietly holding on to each other for a moment, allowing the peace of the night to slip in around them.

"I always wanted a home. I think I convinced myself that home would be a place that would be mine and there wouldn't be any change. I...I realized tonight that

I've never had people over to my home here. I only have a couple of co-workers who I would ever meet out, but never had fun with them the way I have the past couple of days."

She leaned back to stare at his eyes, reaching up to cup his jaw. "Momma was right. Home's gotta be with people you care about." Sighing heavily, she continued, "I wanted the job with GMS, but now? It all seems so tainted."

Kissing her forehead, he said, "You've had a lot going on, baby. Let's go to bed and get a good night's sleep. Things will seem clearer in the morning." *He hoped his words were true and her thoughts would include him.*

Grinning over her shoulder, she looked up into his concerned face. "I'd love to go to bed now…but not sure sleep is on my mind."

Throwing his head back in laughter, he turned her in his arms as he led the way down the hall. "Well, let's see if we can give you something to occupy your time tonight besides sleep!"

13

At work the next day, Evie stayed in her office with the door closed almost all morning. She felt no guilt when she spent over two hours researching engineering jobs in Virginia. Pleased with her results, she even threw out a few inquiries and then spent another hour updating her resume. A knock on her door interrupted her queries and she quickly moved to a different screen before calling out, "Enter."

Saul opened the door hesitantly, peeking in before moving into her office. "Hey," he greeted, his voice not as exuberant as usual.

Forcing her greeting to be less cool than she felt, she greeted him in return. He slid into one of her chairs, his gaze nervously jumping around the room before landing on hers. "I just wondered how you were."

"I'm fine, Saul," she replied sincerely. Her mind moved back to Patrick and a secret smile graced her face.

Seeing her relaxed expression, Saul let out a deep breath. "Good, good. I was worried."

Her eyes jumped to his again as she cocked her head in question. "Worried?"

"Yeah, well, you left in such a hurry the other day and have spent the morning behind your closed door."

"And you don't think I have a reason to be upset?"

"Aw, Evelyn. It's just business. Honestly, it's just the way things happen in industry and sales. As an engineer, you've never had to deal with this side of things, but in the sales and delivery of items, things go wrong."

She remained silent and he took that as an invitation to continue to explain. "We once had an entire overseas shipment go down with a sinking cargo ship. Another time, there was a wreck on the highway when one of our delivery trucks turned over and the whole delivery was damaged."

"Why are you telling me this?" she asked softly.

Twisting his hands in his lap, he shook his head sadly. "I just want you to know that shit happens and we can't always control it. Or keep it from happening. Or change it. I don't want to lose you over this."

"Lose me? Threatening to fire me isn't the same as *losing me* if you want to get down to semantics."

Signing heavily again, he nodded. "I told Gary that was a stupid play. None of us want you to leave, but dad...dad is...you gotta understand. This company is dad's whole world. He built it from the ground up, starting about thirty-five years ago. The company's won awards for excellence and he's been written up for donating percentages to charities. He's so proud of it... probably more proud of it than his sons."

At that tidbit of news, she stared at the man in front of her closely, realizing his emotions were giving her more information than the normally confident man gave.

"Gary's the oldest, so he got to be the Vice President. Ed is an old childhood buddy of dad's and so he's the head of production. Dad keeps a tight rein on the company and he'll react poorly to any negativity."

"I still don't understand why you're telling me all of this."

Piercing her eyes with his intent gaze, he said, "I think you're brilliant and this company is lucky to have you. That's the reason dad wanted to keep you and not let you go to any competition even though you had to wait a few months before the engineering position would be available. I just don't want us to lose you."

She nodded hesitantly, considering her words carefully. "I appreciate that, Saul. I was thrilled to get the job offer from GMS, but confess to having been really upset with the threat of dismissal. I'm having to sincerely consider my options at this point."

The sorrowful expression on Saul's face caused her heart to squeeze. He nodded slowly and stood to leave. "Evelyn, sometimes people do things that don't make sense...or seem wrong. But they have their reasons. I just hope you'll stay long enough to see that we really are a good company."

He walked out her door, closing it behind him, and she let go of a breath she had not realized she was holding. Her mind swirled with the information Saul gave her...both the unspoken as well as his actual words.

Back in Virginia, Luke worked on the computer drives that Marc and Cam brought back. He had been contacted by Dane Logan, a former SEAL who had worked with Chris. Jack cleared the path for Luke to work with Chris's computer guy, hoping the two of them together would be able to assist in locating the missing shipment.

You got the drives? Dane messaged.

Working on them now.

I'll send a decoding program that works for me. Developed it when I couldn't find anything else to work.

Luke grinned as he typed, **Appreciate it. Will reciprocate.**

No problem, Dane came back. **Us techs have to stick together.**

A few minutes later, Luke's computer had the download and he ran the drives through the new program, grinning as he realized it gave him more information than his program. Pouring through the data, he moved to his complicated coffee machine and poured another cup. While relaxing against the counter, he heard his computer alert an incoming new message. *Hmm, Dane must have more to say.*

Walking over, he saw it was not Dane, but his mystery assistant. Several months prior, he had been contacted by someone who could see what he was working on and, determining they could be trusted, he allowed them to assist with a case. Keeping their identity hidden, they continued to assist him and he grew fond of whoever was on the other end.

You have a new friend. I hope they can help you.

Chuckling, Luke wondered how the mystery assistant already found out that Dane was in contact with him.

Yes, it's all good.

He waited a moment to see what they would say next.

Run the data through his program, then through the one I sent you for the last case. You will extrapolate more data that way.

Looking at the screen, he realized they were right. Watching the effects for a few minutes, he grinned. *Now, we're getting somewhere.*

You were right. Thanks.

No problem. I hope I'm not being replaced...

Chuckling, Luke shook his head and typed, **No way. I like working with you.**

Good. I'll be seeing you.

Luke pondered that for a few seconds and then typed, **I hope you mean that literally.**

Only silence greeted him for several long minutes. Then, once more, his message alerted again. **You never know. Maybe. At least I hope so.**

With that, Luke knew he had heard the last from the mystery assistant for a while. Sending another thank you to Dane, he began to pour over the data.

That afternoon, Evie knew she needed to get back to work. She had used too much company time looking for other jobs in Virginia. *One way or another, I'm almost finished with this part of the job*, she consoled herself. Pouring over new orders from the military, she realized she needed to make a visit to Ed. *Maybe I can just email my questions to him. Ugh, he rarely answers emails.* Looking at the clock, she hoped she could catch him. It was after five o'clock and as she opened her door, she noticed most employees had left the building.

Feeling guilty at her lack of performance during the day, she decided to stay late and head to the plant offices, hoping Ed would be working late as well. Dreading the conversation with the surly plant manager, she consoled herself with the fact that she only had a few questions to ask. Sliding her phone into her pocket, she headed out the door. Fifteen minutes later, she entered the plant's security door. Normally visiting the production area during the business hours, it was eerily quiet after closing. Walking along the side of the crates and huge machines, she moved toward the stairs leading to Ed's office.

Hearing loud voices near the top of the stairs, she halted, uncertain whether to move forward or not. Hating to interrupt what was obviously an argument, she stood quiet, hoping the parties would leave.

"I know what you've been doing! I can't believe you'd do this to your family!"

The voices retreated and she stayed perfectly still, wondering what to do.

Luke called Monty at home. "Hey, man. I wanted to give you the intel I've uncovered and let you pass it on to Patrick. Using the data from the drives, and assistance from not only Dane but my mystery assistant again, I've found some interesting information."

"Give it to me and I'll contact Patrick."

"Okay, the warehouse is owned by a number of subsidiary companies but, eventually, I found the owner to be listed as Oysten, Inc."

"Oysten? Isn't that the last name of the people who own GMS?"

"Yes, but what's interesting is who we're looking at. And why they want to stay hidden."

After receiving the phone call from Monty, Patrick dialed Evie. *Come on, pick up.* Looking at the time, he saw it was after six o'clock. He knew that she should have been home. "Baby, call me when you get this message."

Seeing her car was not in her condo's parking lot, he turned around and began driving to GMS. On his way, he called Chris. They agreed to meet at GMS and Patrick stepped on the accelerator, churning the few miles up quickly.

Pulling into the parking lot, he immediately spotted her car still parked in its space. He parked next to her and as he got out, Chris came driving up as well.

"What have you got?" he asked, coming up to Patrick.

"Monty called. Seems Luke and Dane came up with a way to dig deeper into the hidden financial assets of the warehouse the missing shipment was directed to. It's owned by an Oysten. Those are Evie's bosses, but we don't know which one. I tried to call her, but she won't pick up. It's not like her to work late...especially now that she's disgusted with them."

Just then Patrick's phone vibrated. He answered after checking to see who was calling. "Evie, where are you?"

"I saw you had called," she whispered.

His eyes jerked to Chris's. "Why are you whispering? Where are you?" he asked again.

"I'm in the plant. I needed to speak to Ed, but when I got here, it was past closing," she continued to whisper. "There are two men arguing and I'm afraid to make myself known, so I moved back closer to the door to call you."

"Who's arguing? Where's the plant?"

"It's the huge building to the left of the offices I work in."

Patrick glanced up locating the group of buildings she was referring to. "Which one?"

"Why are you asking? Where are you?" she returned, still whispering.

"I'm next to your car. Now, which plant building are

142

you in? I don't want you there alone with two people arguing. You need to leave."

"I'm in Building 5A," she replied softly. "Listen, I think the voices have quieted. I'll go see if I can find Ed and then come out."

"I'm coming to you," Patrick said, but realized she had disconnected. Looking at Chris, he said, "I'm going to her."

Chris grinned and said, "Lead the way, man. I'm in."

The two men took off running around the corporate building toward the production area.

Now that it appeared the loud argument had ended, Evie moved up the stairs leading to Ed's office. Lifting her hand to knock on his door, she stumbled backward as it opened briskly. Stunned, she stared into the face of Norman Oysten, with Ed standing several feet behind him.

"What are you doing here?" he growled, his hand reaching out to grab her arm.

In a split second decision, she jumped back out of his reach and turned quickly, running back to the stairs. Hearing a scuffle behind her, she tripped on the stairs as a shot rang out in the vault-like plant, the echo ringing in her ears. *Oh, my God!*

Recovering her footing, she stumbled the rest of the way down, but heard someone shout her name from the top.

"Get back here! Evie, get back here!"

Another shot rang out. This time, a *ping* bounced off a metal container near her head and she threw her body around the corner of a large crate, her heart pounding a staccato in her chest. *Oh, Jesus, oh, Jesus. What have I gotten myself into?*

Hearing the sound of someone clomping down the stairs, she darted between another group of containers, trying to move inaudibly. Glancing down at her heels, she knew she would be better off barefoot. Slipping off one and then the other, she held them in her hands as she continued to wind around the machinery in the large section of the plant.

"I know you're in here," Norman's voice cried out. "You can't escape me."

Norman? Her frightened mind was unable to process the kind man who hired her with the angry visage that greeted her at the top of the stairs and continued to chase her. Knowing her phone was in her pocket, she remembered Patrick's phone call. *Please find me!*

———

Patrick and Chris made their way to Building 5A and had just entered the main door, after Chris circumvented the security door, when the shot rang out. Hearing shouts, they immediately shared a glance and headed full speed toward the back stairs.

"I know you're in here," a man's voice called. "You can't escape me."

Patrick mouthed, "Circle around," with his forefinger swirling in the air and received Chris's nod. The two men split and while Chris headed toward the right back wall, Patrick moved toward the left. Once out of earshot, Chris called 911, apprising them of the situation.

Patrick peeked around a stack of wooden crates and viewed an older man at the bottom of the stairs, holding a gun. The man's eyes were wide and wildly looking around. *Who the hell is that? Ed?* The only person Patrick had met from Evie's work was Saul, and it certainly was not him. *And where the fuck is Evie?*

The man turned and began creeping along the wall away from Patrick. Slipping around the crate stack, Patrick followed him for several yards until he was able to move stealthily behind him.

Hearing a slight noise, he observed Evie slipping around another crate, but unbeknownst to her, she was heading straight for the man with the gun. Wasting no time, he shouted, "Evie! Stop!"

She immediately halted, flattening herself against the side of the crate nearest her. Unable to see what was happening, she trusted Patrick.

As Patrick's voice cried out his warning, the man with the gun whirled around, firing a shot in his general direction. Rushing him, Chris came from the side just as Patrick kicked the armed hand up, sending the weapon flying through the air. Landing on the floor, the gunman crumpled under Chris's weight before Chris jumped up, pulling the man with him.

"Evie! Evie!" Patrick yelled. "Come out! We've got him!"

Evie's body flew around the crates, slamming into

Patrick's. He took her weight effortlessly as she jumped into his arms. Holding her shaking body closely to his, with one arm under her ass and the other cradling her head, he realized he was quaking as much as she.

Running footsteps were heard behind them and Patrick jerked around, setting Evie down quickly and shoving her behind his body.

"Police!" a voice shouted, as members of the SPD came into view.

Lifting his hands in the air, Patrick called out. "We called you. We've apprehended the shooter."

"The person he shot is upstairs," Evie said, her hands holding on tightly to Patrick's waist. She watched as several policemen and EMTs ran up the stairs. "I don't know for sure who he shot," she whispered. "But I think it was Ed. They were the ones arguing."

Chris handed Norman over to the police, as Patrick and Evie began answering their questions. She stood on rubbery legs, but with Patrick's arm around her, she steeled her spine, realizing the two of them could face anything.

Just then, more shouting was heard and once again, Patrick moved Evie protectively behind him. Saul and Gary ran from one of the outside entrances and skidded to a halt as they came upon the group.

"Oh, dad," Saul cried, as Evie looked on, stupefied at the events.

14

Sitting in a bar several hours later, Cherylenne had joined her husband at the table he shared with Patrick and Evie.

"Norman? The company's owner?" Cherylenne asked, sipping her beer and eyeing the plate of wings that had been served.

Evie, still reeling from the day's events, nodded. "Yes, it appears that he began siphoning a small portion of some of the shipments to the military bases over twenty years ago during the Gulf war. He found it a lucrative way to have a side business. He knew the military's budget would pay top dollar and he would undercut some of his competitor's bids to get the contracts. Then, he'd make up the difference and more by selling some on the black market."

"Un-fucking-believable," Chris announced.

Patrick grinned at his friend and, slapping him on the back, said, "Gotta thank you for having my back today. You and Dane, both, really helped us tremendously."

"I just can't believe it was him. At all our meetings, he was…well, not meek…but certainly not a gun-toting madman! And to think that I thought it was Ed."

Cherylenne, still trying to catch up, asked, "So Ed was the one who got shot?"

Nodding, Patrick said, "Yeah. It seems that Ed had been doing some investigating himself—"

"And the sons, Gary and Saul," Evie piped up, interrupting.

"Whoa!" Cherylenne exclaimed.

Patrick continued, "Saul, being in charge of the finances, knew something was happening. He talked to Gary and, together with Ed, they began their own investigation into what was going on. From what Saul told the police, they suspected their father, but hadn't been able to prove what he was doing."

"And then I came along," Evie added, "and threw a kink into their plans. They wanted to keep me out of things because they were afraid I would find out what was happening first. If they discovered the truth, they would deal with their dad quietly. You know, have him retire gracefully and no one would know of their dad's illegal dealings."

Patrick growled, "They shouldn't have threatened you. Even if they were trying to stop their dad, that was an asshole maneuver."

Nodding, Evie agreed. "Yeah, but I guess it must be weird to think that their dad was stealing and dealing on the black market."

The foursome finished their meal and leaned back, enjoying the music. After a few minutes, the two women headed to the ladies' room. Chris looked over at Patrick and asked, "So, do you know what you're going to do in a month when you get out?"

Patrick shot a glance in the direction where Evie had walked, his mind on the beauty in his life. Before he had a chance to respond, Chris continued, "'Cause if you stay, I can easily send some investigations your way."

Responding honestly, he said, "I guess I've got a lot of thinking to do."

———————

That night, Evie laid in Patrick's arms, the joyous sounds of their lovemaking having faded into the quiet darkness. Neither slept…neither talked. Both lost in their own thoughts. Finally, he rolled over, facing her. "I was terrified tonight, babe," he confessed. "I heard that gunshot and, swear to God, no matter how many times I've heard gunfire in training and in battle…that one sound nearly undid me."

"I was scared too," she admitted. "I was just so stunned and then ran…as though on instinct."

"The survival instinct is strong…as is the protection instinct. Especially when the heart is involved."

Smiling a shy smile, she stared into his blue eyes, barely discernable in the soft moonlight through the window. Her gaze roamed his face, taking in the stubbled jaw and strong lips. Leaning in closer, she whispered, "And is your heart involved?"

His hand cupped the side of her face as he moved his thumb over the soft skin of her cheek before dragging over her smiling lips. "Yeah, babe. My heart's as involved with you as it can possibly be. You gotta know…I love you, Evie."

Her smile widened as his lips met hers before she was able to say the words back to him. So she let her kiss speak for her. And then she let her body show him once more.

Two days later, Evie looked up from her desk and could see Gary and Saul disappearing into Saul's office. Standing, she followed them and, knocking on the doorframe, announced her presence.

"Come on in, Evelyn," Saul called out. "We're discussing the company and you need to hear what we're discussing."

She entered, settling in one of the comfortable leather chairs and gazed at both men. Remembering the last time she was in the room with both of them, she now wondered what they were going to speak to her about.

"Evelyn, I need to begin with an apology," Gary confessed, his expression remorseful. "I behaved abominably, but truly felt trapped. We," he nodded to his brother, "had been trying to find out what was going on and just wanted to keep everyone else out of it."

Irritation flew through her and she bit out, "Yes, but if you had alerted the authorities earlier, your father might only be facing charges dealing with the thefts… not attempted murder."

The two brothers winced at her words, but each knew she spoke the truth.

"How is Ed, by the way?" she asked.

"He's going to be fine," Saul answered. "Thank God." He shared a look with Gary before proceeding. "Evelyn, the reason we wanted to talk to you, besides to apologize, was to say that we now need you more than ever. The news has raced through the plant and we have had quite a few resignations…people wanting to jump off the ship—"

"Before it goes down?" she bit out, cocking her head to the side.

"No, no," Saul assured. "GMS is still financially sound. We've just got to weather the bad press and can then move forward."

"Anyway," Gary interrupted, "we're ready for you to start immediately as an engineer. There will be a new office, a new area for you to work in, obviously a huge increase in salary. We see you as becoming our lead engineer very quickly."

The room was quiet for a moment as Evie weighed her options. She already knew her heart, but did not want to make a rash decision. Shaking her head, she held back a grin. *Who am I kidding? Time for the cautious Evie to move forward!*

Standing, she smoothed down her skirt before lifting her gaze first to Gary and then to Saul. "Gentlemen, I want to thank you for the faith you have in me, but I think you are over-optimistic if you think that this company won't suffer. While you'll come out in the press as the ones who tried to oust your father, you will find that not many companies, nor the military, will be quick to order from you. And while I do agree that my engineering skills could be of significant value to GMS, I have decided to resign...effective immediately."

Turning toward the door, she had not yet walked through it when Saul's voice called out to her. "Evie... I'm sorry."

Glancing back over her shoulder, she offered him a sincere smile. "I'm not, Saul. For the first time in my life, I'm willing to take a chance...and it feels great."

Placing a quick phone call, she moved back to her office and packed her personal belongings, which fit easily in her large tote. Taking a last look around, she walked down the hall, stopping at the door to turn in her security badge to the guard at the front.

Stepping out into the California sunshine, she slid her sunglasses onto her face and smiled at the handsome man leaning against his jeep. With his military uniform sleeves rolled up, his muscular arms strained at the material. One leg crossed in front of the other, she viewed his booted feet up to his short haircut. Unable to see his eyes, covered with reflector sunglasses, she smiled anyway, knowing they were directed at her.

Patrick watched the beauty walk toward him, her smile piercing his heart. She did not stop until her shoes were directly in front of his boots. Standing to his full height, he reached his hands out to her shoulders. Holding her for a moment, he slipped her sunglasses up her face, pulling her hair back at the same time.

Wanting to peer into her eyes, he slid his glasses up as well.

"Anything you want to tell me?" he asked, hope pounding in his chest.

"Thought I'd tell you that I'm officially unemployed...I quit!"

Laughing, he picked her up, twirling her in celebration.

Giggling, Evie confessed, "I should be upset but, honestly? It feels great!"

Setting her back down, he assisted her into his jeep. "Let's grab something to eat and you can tell me all about it."

Agreeing, she told him about her meeting over lunch. Munching on the last of her French Fries, she said, "So, I'm unemployed and for the first time in my life, I'm not sure what my plan is."

Leaning over to kiss the side of her lips, Patrick said, "Babe, we've built something amazing between us. I'd protect you with my life. And it's no secret I want us to be together. So, if you want to stay in California, we can both look for jobs here."

Her heart leaped in her throat at Patrick's willingness to alter his life plans for her. Her hand moved to cup his jaw as she stared deeply into his sincere expression. "I left GMS today...not only because I wanted to quit working for them, but because of another reason."

Patrick held his breath, awaiting her to continue.

"And, since I plan on moving to Virginia with you, I can hardly commute to California!"

It took a second for her words to sink in. "Moving? You'll move with me? Across the country?" he yelled.

"Yes, yes," she laughed. Before she had a chance to speak further, he leaned in to kiss her again. This time, much more than a sweet kiss—this kiss was claiming— and she felt it down to her toes.

Finally pulling apart, remembering they were in a restaurant, she continued to smile, holding his gaze. "After all," she said, "I can't let go of the man I love."

"I love you too, baby," Patrick enthused. Quickly paying, he ushered her back to his jeep. "Let's get you home."

Agreeing, she added, "Home for now...but not for long."

Four weeks later, Chris and Cherylenne stood outside of Evie's condo, saying goodbye. A moving company had left several hours earlier with her furniture and Patrick's, and now his jeep held just what they would need for their cross-country sojourn.

"So how long will it take you?" Cherylenne asked.

"We're going to make some sight-seeing stops along the way before ending up in North Carolina to see my mom and sister," Evie explained. "Then we'll head to Virginia."

"You going with Jack's group of Saints?" Chris asked Patrick.

Nodding, Patrick confirmed, "Yep. I've already been

in contact with him and we're all set. I'll start with them officially in about three weeks."

"And what about you?" Chris asked Evie.

Smiling, she replied, "It seems that one of the Saints has a fiancé that works in a factory nearby and she says they're desperate for engineers. I'll give them a try."

With the last box loaded, they hugged their friends goodbye and settled into the jeep. Pulling out onto the highway, Patrick looked over at Evie.

"You ready for a new adventure?" he asked.

"Oh yeah. And you?" she countered.

"Babe, with what we have built?" Repeating the words of his grandfather, he said, "We take care of this, cherish it, protect it…it'll last a lifetime."

Get ready for the next Saint!
Remember Love

Don't miss any news about new releases! Sign up for my Newsletter

Cael

Jaxon

Jayden

Asher

Zeke

Cas

Lighthouse Security Investigations

Mace

Rank

Walker

Drew

Blake

Tate

Levi

Clay

Cobb

Hope City (romantic suspense series co-developed
with Kris Michaels

Brock book 1

Sean book 2

Carter book 3

Brody book 4

Kyle book 5

Ryker book 6

Rory book 7

Killian book 8

Torin book 9

Saints Protection & Investigations

(an elite group, assigned to the cases no one else wants…or can solve)

Serial Love

Healing Love

Revealing Love

Seeing Love

Honor Love

Sacrifice Love

Protecting Love

Remember Love

Discover Love

Surviving Love

Celebrating Love

Searching Love

Follow the exciting spin-off series:

Alvarez Security (military romantic suspense)

Gabe

Tony

Vinny

Jobe

SEALs

Thin Ice (Sleeper SEAL)

SEAL Together (Silver SEAL)

Undercover Groom (Hot SEAL)

Also for a Hope City Crossover Novel / Hot SEAL...

A Forever Dad by Maryann Jordan

Letters From Home (military romance)

Class of Love

Freedom of Love

Bond of Love

The Love's Series (detectives)

Love's Taming

Love's Tempting

Love's Trusting

The Fairfield Series (small town detectives)

Emma's Home

Laurie's Time

Carol's Image

Fireworks Over Fairfield

Please take the time to leave a review of this book. Feel free to contact me, especially if you enjoyed my book. I love to hear from readers!

Facebook

Email

Website

ABOUT THE AUTHOR

I am an avid reader of romance novels, often joking that I cut my teeth on the historical romances. I have been reading and reviewing for years. In 2013, I finally gave into the characters in my head, screaming for their story to be told. From these musings, my first novel, Emma's Home, The Fairfield Series was born.

I was a high school counselor having worked in education for thirty years. I live in Virginia, having also lived in four states and two foreign countries. I have been married to a wonderfully patient man for thirty-five years. When writing, my dog or one of my four cats can generally be found in the same room if not on my lap.

Please take the time to leave a review of this book. Feel free to contact me, especially if you enjoyed my book. I love to hear from readers!

Facebook
Email
Website

Made in the USA
Coppell, TX
21 January 2022

72059552R00100